ANGEL OF VAPE

Melvin Provario

The following *never* happened. Wink wink.

For your eyes only

Special Agent Lance Pleasant
Federal Bureau of Investigation
Violent Crimes Against Children

Dear Special Agent Pleasant,

Enclosed and without redaction are the exhibits, four handwritten letters. Please be advised that the protocols regarding this matter have remained unchanged and assume as much for the foreseeable future. The classification on this case is classified, so treat Core Secret.

To refresh your memory, during October of last year a series of gruesome murders perplexed the country. Two related men, one Phil Zigfield and one Larry Zigfield, were tortured and killed in separate incidents in the city of Chicago. It came to the attention of investigators that a third relative, Daniel Zigfield, who was living in a southwestern suburb, had also been tortured and murdered. This prompted the reopening of the investigation of the death of *yet another* relative. Roger Zigfield's death was initially ruled an accident but signs of foul play were then uncovered in that case as well. This bizarre string of crimes prompted the exhumation of one Bartholomew Zigfield, who, during the same period of time, was thought to have died of lung cancer. The postmortem autopsy revealed that Mr. Zigfield's remains contained approximately 147 milligrams of nicotine per kilogram. The medium lethal dosage of nicotine in adults is .5 to 1 mg/kg. The medical examiner was quoted, "If you smoked this man's flesh, you would absorb more nicotine than you would if you smoked a filterless cigarette."

Both the Mayor of Chicago and the newly elected Governor of Illinois proclaimed their resolve to bring the culprit(s) to justice, and so there was much pressure to solve the case. Human rights activists have expressed the concern that this pressure produced an unproductive atmosphere that tainted the investigation, that the investigators were more concerned with saving face by producing a suspect than they were with finding out the truth. It was out of this atmosphere that, based on an anonymous tip and at the request of local authorities, federal agents raided the nicotine extraction laboratory of one Jerry Little of Ford Heights, where they found electronic cigarette paraphernalia similar to items discovered at the scenes of the various crimes, including: hollowed out knick-knacks called "drip tips" (used for the smoking of electronic cigarettes); kanthal electrical wiring (typically used as the heating element in e-cigarette); electronic gadgets and contraptions designed to produce e-cig vapors; bottles of vegetable glycerin and propylene glycol (ingredients for the liquid used in e-cigs); as well as concentrated nicotine solutions. Jerry Little was apprehended and ultimately charged with five counts of first degree murder and after an unusually speedy trial, he was found guilty on all counts and received five consecutive life sentences. Three weeks after trial, Jerry Little was found hanging by the neck in his cell from a knotted rope he allegedly made from strips of material from his own garments.

It has come to our attention that prior to Jerry Little's apparent suicide, our Illinois task force received, by means of standard mail, four envelopes containing the following letters purported to be authored by one Melvin Provario. These letters were mailed to an undercover safe house that was occasionally being used for sting operation targeting online predators. The letters were addressed only to the word "Yugo" with no return address. The parcels were overlooked and were not opened and inspected until after the death of Jerry Little.

I can't stress enough the sensitivity of this matter. If the information contained in these letters were to be released to the public prematurely, consider the following:

1. Although it is not the Bureau's obligation to protect the reputation of public officials, it is also not the Bureau's habit to haphazardly act to destroy those reputations. Releasing this information without being absolutely certain about its origin and authenticity would destroy the reputations of those who would be held accountable for what will be perceived as the conviction and subsequent death of an innocent man.

2. The reputation of this Division and the Bureau itself would come under scrutiny, with the suggestion that evidence that may have exonerated an innocent man was in our possession, but was ignored until it was too late to act upon it.

3. The amount of civil litigation that would follow the release of this information is estimated to be in the millions.

4. Public anxiety ignited by these crimes, eased only after the apprehension of the suspect, would be stirred up again, upon the suggestion that the perpetrator is at large. We believe your investigation would run smoother without the interference of public scrutiny.

5. We believe, if the contents of these envelopes are genuine, the perpetrator delivered them to the Division of Violent Crimes Against Children by mistake. If so, we believe he is presently relaxed and not in hiding. If it is revealed to him that you are in possession of this material, the perpetrator will be given a heads up and he will then actively elude you.

6. If these letters prove genuine, the Bureau believes the perpetrator can be apprehended under alternative pretexts and charged with and convicted of any number of crimes. We believe you will be able to get the perpetrator into custody and bring him to justice without any mention of the Zigfield murders. The goal should be to get <u>Melvin Provario</u> off the street, not to create irreversible scandal.

It is the advice of this Office that the investigation of Melvin Provario should remain an internal matter and should be treated with the highest level of confidentiality. It is therefore requested that, under no circumstance during your investigation, not during any interview, nor in any written or electronic correspondence, should the Zigfield murders be alluded to.

Yours sincerely,

Desi Shiftlett
Office of Crisis Management

Burn after reading

ANGEL OF VAPE: VAPE MANIA 2

FIRST WRAP: Cloud Chasing

Dear Yugo,

It was through sheer coincidence that I uncovered your contact information. I found a postcard promoting your web cam service on the floor near the urinal of a certain video store I occasionally patronize, and even though you are going under the name Suzy Sampler I recognized you by your photo. In it I believe you are wearing the same pleated skirt you were wearing the day we met—is that true? I was sorry to see that your site had been shut down before I could get to it, but a few months ago I was able to trace the snail mail address associated with your domain name, so that is where I will be sending these letters.

The reason I didn't contact you sooner is because I have so much to say and I feel I need to put my thoughts in order so that I might be able to explain myself fully. Be assured that even though our time together was brief, you have always been on my mind. Once you understand the circumstances leading up to what I've done, you can either choose to forgive me, then perhaps we can find a means to share a life together (this is what I believe was our destiny since the moment I set eyes on you, when we were vaping Cookie Monsta juice on the bench in the park) or you can choose not to, and I will understand, considering how grave my situation is. I will not beat around the bush. I have murdered five people. But I can explain.

Since you know me, I will assume you'll expect me to be frank and not hold back any details. I want to say that it all started at the Vaporee Festival, but the powers in play may have been working on me even before that. This was the situation I found myself in. At one end of the exhibitor's hall stood Damian, wearing a dark red Blackhawk's jersey. He was puffing defiantly on a big stogie protruding from his puckered lips like a turd stuck in a constipated anus, his bulbous nose above it like the hemorrhoid causing the blockage. He seemed to relish his demonstration of contempt for vaping by blowing his sickeningly sweet carbon and tar into Vaporee's first downtown Chicago gathering. His smoke was going unnoticed though, in the large open room partitioned into aisles between vendor tables, where everyone was vaping and blowing clouds like a bubbling hot spring.

I am going to assume that you've read the book called *Vape Mania*. If not, perhaps you should read it before you continue. I want to make it perfectly clear that the notes that are documented in that book were heavily molested by the Institute for the Preservation of the Institution of Cigarettes (IPIC). I never used the simile "like a shot deer" to describe the time when I had to drag Damian's girlfriend Melany up a flight of stairs. If you ask me, the definition of consent has been skewed these days, but nevertheless, I kept my head down, the brim of my trilby so tight over my forehead that the hat shifted with the movement of my eyebrows. My Fu Manchu mustache had fallen off twice already and was barely clinging to the flesh above my upper lip, its glue failing further with every fluttering breath from my nostrils. I edged sideways, table by table, away from Damian, who was standing there perusing the room patiently; my hope was that he would see nothing but a hat on top of my long trench coat, a coat that had maintained a maroon tint to it after an accident involving a Jacuzzi full of e-juice.

At the other end of the exhibitor's hall, Mike Crow was snooping around, with his laminated press-pass flopping under his white boy dreadlocks with an arrogant purpose from a rope around his neck as he held his flashing camera as if it was an Oscar. If I tried to make it to the south exit I would run into him, the most notorious of the Vaporazzi. He would love to get a snapshot of me, the infamous Melvin Provario, alleged author of that ridiculous book that had been hacked to pieces by Big Tobacco prior to its publication; but if I made my way to the north exit, I risked being found out by the monomaniac who was there to do me great bodily harm over his girlfriend's own lack of judgment.

"Five dollar cartos," yapped the beady eyed pumpkin face sporting an orange Mohawk, who mistook my attempts at being incognito with interest in what he was peddling at his table.

"What's so special about that?" I asked. "Cartos like this usually run five bucks."

"But these are the bomb," he said. I strained my eyes to find his miniscule mouth lost within his fat face as I approached, flipping the collar of my trench coat over my jaw. Lining his table were hundreds of metal tubes, each about the length and width of my pinky. Some were painted in psychedelic fashion, some were stainless steel with designs etched into them, and still others had holographic images stamped onto them.

"Hmm. These *are* nice cartos," I agreed. "But what's the point?"

When the man shrugged, his head sunk down instead of his shoulders rising. "What do you mean what's the point?"

"I mean, cartos like these are disposable." I pointed to one. "That's merely a metal tube wrapped around an atomizer with some filler material in it. Even with a carto tank, you can use it for perhaps a week or two before the filler is shot and then what?"

"Not true," he said as if blowing his words out of a straw. "You can boil them and dry them in the oven and they're as good as new."

"I'm sure you can get away with that a few times," I argued, "but that's about it. That one there, the nice one with the hologram of a bird on it for example — wouldn't that hologram get destroyed if you boiled it?"

"Well what do you want for five dollars!" the man shot.

I thought about that for a moment and surrendered, "You have a point there," and I searched my many coat pockets until I found a crinkled five dollar bill and gave it to the man as I snatched up the 3D bird cartomizer. I pulled a bottle of Pomegranate e-juice from my breast pocket and unscrewed the cap and primed the filler, but as always I suffered from carto-impatience and squirted in too much and it started leaking out the 510 connector. The pumpkin man handed me a strip of paper towel and I dabbed the connector until it stopped leaking and then I screwed it to a C-twist and then popped on an Eiffel Tower drip tip and then had a warm vape that started blowing out of my nose before I was finished sucking it in.

"Dual coil," the pumpkin said.

"Dual coil?" I solicited with a nod of satisfaction.

"One point four ohms," he said with an open smile as if there was a puppy's ear between his cheeks.

"Really?" I yielded and took another toot, relishing it. "Well, sir, I do believe that's the best five bucks I've ever spent."

"Thank you, sir."

"Now, if you'll excuse me," I said, acting as if I was bending over to tie my shoe, but as I crouched down below the waistline of the mingling crowd, I fell to my shoulder and rolled under the banner that draped his table. I hid there in the shadows near the man's crotch smell as Damian's combat boots passed one way and Mike Crow's thrift store Converse painted neon pink went the other way.

I crawled on my palms and toes as silently and slowly as a cat stalking a mouse, hidden by the hanging table cloths that sported vendor names, catching a glimpse of someone's abacus clitoral hood jewelry, then some calloused hand with dirt under its fingernails, shifting a misplaced testicle with stealthy nudges from a middle finger, enduring someone else's cheek sneak cheese and alcohol silencer, all the while maneuvering between knees and table cloths so as not be discovered traversing the length of the exhibit hall beneath the tables.

To my astonishment I was not alone in my narrow route of escape. Three tables ahead of me I saw a young woman sitting Indian style, dull light shining through the thick black spectacles on the face of the logo on the frilly Happy Potter Vapery banner draped over the table above her. She had short hair dyed light pink and striking green eyes that peeked through minute slits as if she was born with a permanent squint. Black plastic bats with their wings spread hung from her earlobes and her almost non-existent breasts were scrunched up under her Ramones t-shirt by her crouch, protruding just slightly out from between the zipper and snaps of her black leather jacket. As I came closer like a wolf creeping toward a herd of sheep I suddenly froze, thinking for the moment that it might be you.

"Yugo?" I asked, my voice trembling.

She turned and grimaced at me. "No," she whispered. I remained on all fours, frozen and staring at her until she said, "Elle."

"What are you doing, Elle?" I whispered back.

"Hiding. What does it look like?" she said with a mixture of irritation and inquisitiveness.

"So am I," I whispered.

"I can see that," she said, offering a slight smile.

I slithered between the legs of a flimsy table that kept wobbling around from whatever they were doing on it and I silently plopped down on my side near her. I was next to a pair of skinny bare female legs wearing Scooby-Doo socks and she was next to someone who had removed his prosthetic leg and had it leaning against his muscular one that was tattooed like a graphic novel.

She shook her head, growing increasingly amused by me, and she rolled her eyes and sort of slapped her palms onto her legs and asked, "What do you have to vape?"

"How old are you?" I asked in return.

"I'm eighteen," she assured me.

"I don't believe you," I replied.

She huffed and grasped her purse that was shoved in her leg well and rummaged through it until she found an ID card and she held it up for me defiantly. I struggled to read it in the dim shadows and when I finally did, I said, "Aha! You won't be eighteen until tomorrow!"

"You mean in eight hours!"

"That's the law," I said with finality. "Here," and I squirmed around, balancing on an elbow to retrieve a business card from the inside hip pocket of my coat. I bumped my head against the bottom of the table, sending it wobbling, at which point we both froze wide eyed, waiting to see if we were discovered; for Elle, wide eyed meant slightly more open than those of someone under the effects of morphine, although this is not to suggest her eyes weren't sober in their slits. I handed her the card.

"Dirty Vape Operations," she read, the tension in her body melting. "Strictly off the books!"

"Look me up in eight hours," I said. "Now, I hate to tell you this, but I have to get by, so either you'll have to move or —"

"Okay, go ahead," she said, and she lied on her back like a plank, remaining stiff and still as I crawled over her. I found myself completely on top of her, my face inches from her face.

"Please don't panic," I sighed with a cringe. "It's just that I'm getting a cramp in my ribcage." She rolled her head up and down on the floor. My Fu Manchu mustache released its grip and flopped down onto her face like a big spider. She puckered her lips and whistled at it and it danced around before falling away. I managed to get an arm moving and pulled myself forward, when it dawned upon me that if I took a couple more crawling steps, she would find herself face to face with my manhood. Imagining that she may panic and strike me, sending the table above us overturning as we struggled through the misunderstanding, I hissed in discomfort, "Maybe you want to get on your side and sort of ssslink out." As if playing Twister, the two of us spent the next few minutes getting untangled from each other in a slow, tedious but masterful way that didn't inspire any suspicion from above.

Finally I was freed from the dilemma and made my way under the next table. I peeked out from under the vendor's cloth and could see the exit sign. "For what it's worth," I whispered back at Elle, "in eight hours, I'll most likely be in love with you." She shrugged her shoulders not knowing how to respond, with my card still gripped between her fingers. I dashed out from under the table and managed a swift walking run toward the exit with my head bowed and my hand crushing my trilby over my face.

When I escaped out into the late afternoon sun, I searched my trench coat for my new holographic carto, and not finding it, discovered that Elle was a rather masterful pickpocket.

At the time, I was renting the attic of a two-story single family frame home on South Canalport Avenue from Brandon Bieberman, who had no authority to rent me anything since his two fathers were merely travelling across India for the summer in an attempt to rekindle their relationship. The funny thing is that I had noticed the house on more than one occasion while hitchhiking on 90/94. For years the house had a blue plastic tarp nailed to a section of the peaked shingle roof, the edges of which would flap around with the wind, and I often wondered why nobody bothered to fix whatever the problem was, since the rest of the house was well kept with white wide paneled steel siding and double pane vinyl windows. Last summer, I found myself living under that very hole in the roof, under the very tarp that made the attic glow blue when it was sunny out and that gave off a noisy racket like jazz rakes when it got rained on.

Brandon explained that the year the White Sox won the world series a few of the players managed to commandeer the Good Year Blimp and were having a champagne party with some high end escorts, when everyone moved to one side too swiftly causing the airship to sway, sending a large crystal bowl of guacamole sliding out of the window of the hull, where it came spinning down reflecting sunlight like a meteor ejecting a green tail; and it crashed through the roof of the Bieberman house. The repairs would be put on hold indefinitely during a prolonged battle to determine if the Ball Club or if the Tire and Rubber Company was liable, and the two Mr. Biebermans were in no rush to mend the house, since doing so would set a firm value on the damage and they knew no matter who was liable, the settlement promised to be most lucrative. Someone could have been killed by that bowl of guacamole, after all.

Nine years after the flying saucer of avocado blasted through the roof, I found myself living in what was basically a crawlspace. I could only stand straight in the very center, under the tip of the peak; anywhere else and I had to duck in order to avoid the sharp nails that protruded through the sheathing. There was no floor, merely sheets of thin plywood strewn haphazardly, some of them overlapping each other, on top of beams with piles of dirty gray insulation between them, the drywall ceiling of the second floor just below that. I found it symbolic that I should be living in the house that was avocado bombed by the White Sox, since I too was waiting upon a settlement in my lawsuit against the tobacco advocacy group that had managed to get ahold of my private vaping notes. As I said, they had edited my writing horribly before marketing it to the public without my permission. The lawsuit was all formality, since it was clear cut that my rights were violated, according to Goldstein, Silverberg and Pearlman, the firm I found on the back cover of the yellow pages. All I needed to do was do nothing, be patient and wait, and one day I would get a settlement check, minus their forty percent of course.

The attic could be accessed from a square trap in the ceiling of the rear porch, a trap that was just slightly wider than the width of my shoulders, only by climbing up an aluminum ladder leaning against the trap's frame and only by lifting through like a gymnast on a balance beam. Inside the attic near the trap was a tiny window through which I often saw Brandon decked out in a white jumpsuit and enormous sneakers, dancing to Milli Vanilli, jerking his arms around like a cheerleader, with a big dollar sign made out of fake gold bouncing around on his chest from a thick chain, in the backyard near the apple tree where he often pulled out a set of stereo speakers and set up a tall, narrow mirror against the neighbor's six foot privacy fence. Sometimes I sat there on a milk crate vaping Dolphin Sauce from Baker Hill out of a Vivi Nova 2.5 attached to a mechanical mod watching Brandon dance for hours; sometimes he looked like Dolph Lundgren trying to walk on hot coals, and sometimes he looked like Evel Knievel crashing when went down on a square of cardboard and attempted to breakdance.

Brandon stood six feet tall, had six pack abs, kept his hair combed up in a tall, hair sprayed formation and had a deformed mouth that pointed to the left with absurdly plumb lips that seemed to snarl. His freakish mouth didn't come off as grotesque, but instead accentuated his all too serious white boy face as if he was the direct spawn of some mutated Elvis sperm. As odd of a bird as he was, he wasn't alone in this world like I was, so he must have been doing something right.

With the help of some rope I managed to pull up two kitchen chairs, a futon mattress, an end table that got damaged in the process and had to be duct taped back together, a lamp and various other items that I found in the alleys. It was a good enough cubbyhole to hide in while certain distractions in my life ironed themselves out, and Brandon only charged me $75 a month for it. I assured him that since I'm a vaper and not a smoker, there was no chance of me setting the place on fire, and he was genuinely interested and thought my mods were cool.

During my time in the attic I suffered a severe bout of paranoia, so I spent a good deal of time hiding there beneath the rafters among the cobwebs and electrical wiring. To explain what triggered this, I need to go back to that day at the Vaporee Festival.

I was hiding under the vendor's tables, having just met Elle, a girl quite literally on the verge of womanhood, when I decided to make a break for it and roll out from under the hanging table cloth, but in my haste toward the exit sign I neglected to scope the room, and I heard from behind me an angry voice shout, "Hey! Stop right there!" followed by some shuffling and complaining and cursing that I could only imagine was Damian forcing his way through the dense crowd in pursuit of me. Instead of heading toward the exit, I instinctually dashed toward the main stage, where there was a marathon cloud chasing contest taking place. One contestant was blowing a cloud produced from a certain Kayfun clone while another was blowing a cloud from a different Kayfun clone, while judges sitting on the sidelines documented the impressiveness of the clouds by marking score cards. I held my trilby firmly to my head so as not to lose it as I sprung headfirst like someone pushing an automobile out of the snow, plunging into the vanilla fog and like a Las Vegas magic act, as the vapor dissipated, I had vanished, to the bewilderment of my pursuer. Of course I wasn't vanished at all, but was hiding behind a partition where electrical cables hung amongst ropes and pulleys and sandbags. As quiet as a bird, I crept down an extremely narrow set of stairs and found myself beneath the stage, hearing feet stomping above me. Someone shouted, "Do you mind?" before the

21

smoke alarms were tripped for the fifteenth time that day. The first time the smoke alarms went off that morning, the sprinklers came on giving us all a shower; after the event organizers argued with the hotel staff, insisting the nature of the vaping festival had been disclosed completely and honestly in advance, the management agreed to deactivate the sprinklers but for safety reason could not deactivate the alarms. The question of how e-cig vapor, that doesn't contain smoke, was setting off the smoke detectors, well, I can't explain, but that's what happened about twice an hour throughout the day; and so once again, as I hid under the stage, the Vaporee organizers were having a heated argument with the hotel manager.

I couldn't exactly climb back up and pop my head out because Damian was most likely still lingering, scratching his head like a dolt who had been hoodwinked, looking here and there in vain. I managed to find some hanging light bulbs and I pulled their chains and I searched around the stage's underbelly that was basically a gigantic box that had some stage props and music stands and podiums and sound equipment stored in it. I found what promised to be the only exit, a manhole cover that I pried open using a microphone stand. The vaping festival was being held in the bottom sub-floor of the hotel, so I could only imagine where this hole would take me, but at the moment any alternative was better than being pummeled by the man who was convinced that I had date raped and impregnated his girlfriend. So down I went, but to my horror my foot went into a free fall as I tried to catch the next nonexistent rung, and I fell, hanging by one hand, gripping the rusted remnants of a ladder that had rotted away years ago. I could hear rats screeching and water trickling below me as I hung in the blackness, desperately trying to pull myself up, but the sharp, corroded rung I held onto dug into my palm and my grip failed. I went down, landing with a splash into a tunnel made of bricks, a bit of light coming from the manhole that was beyond my reach.

I immediately accepted that my situation was dire. I was alone, trapped in a rat infested sewer, with nowhere to go except into complete darkness. I remembered I was carrying a White Fog Mega Bling cigalike that I won in a Wheel of Vapor spin earlier in the day. The Mega Bling is a plastic cigar, twice the size of the Bling and four times the size of the Bling Mini. I rummaged through my many trench coat pockets until I found it and I ripped its wrapper off with my teeth. When I put it to my mouth and sucked, the end of it lit up, revealing for those vaping seconds what existed before me as my mouth was filled with the taste of chocolate and mint. "Hmmmm," I said to myself, "not bad," and my words echoed in the dungeon. The Mega Bling boasted that it was equal to four packs of cigarettes, and I sure hoped that wasn't an exaggeration, because if it had a faulty battery I would be left with no source of light whatsoever.

Each time I took a puff the sewer was revealed, allowing me to trudge through the questionable, lumpy slime that smelled like ammonia. I only took puffs when I absolutely was unsure of what stood before me in order to conserve the battery. My Yugo, I don't think I need to emphasize how terrifying this was; you need only imagine yourself in this circumstance, but I kept my cool by imagining I was playing an old Super Nintendo version of Wizardry in which only a few blocks of the dungeon are revealed with each step.

As more rats splashed and squeaked, I took a big pull on the Bling and found myself face to face with an enormous spider spread out on its web like an asterisk. I was taken aback and my Bling fell out of my mouth and by some miracle of reflex I caught it in my hand before it went into the muck. "You don't want to do that!" I told myself and put the Bling back, holding it firmly between my teeth, sucking and maneuvering around the eight legged freak. I imagined there might be snakes squirming around, and I started moaning like a soiled child, tiptoeing and lighting the way with every drag. My heart began beating with panic as time and distance increased with no end to the tunnel in site. As if through a voice pipe, I could hear the roar of flushing water followed by rushing yellow foam at my feet. As I sucked in more vapor to light my way, my head began spinning and I grew nauseas. I was overdosing on nicotine. Oh why did I have to choose the XX-Strength Mega Bling as my prize!

There was some more flushing and as the foamy muck began to rise a desperate rat tried to crawl up my pants. I shook my leg in panic, screaming like a horror queen, and it seemed spiders were landing on my face. There were more flushing sounds and my shoes started slipping in the stream as the current picked up and heavy, sopping wet wads of paper fell down from somewhere and slapped against my hat and coat as I attempted to dodge them; and the floor began to decline and several flushes happened all at once like thunder clapping and as I sucked on my Bling *yes!* there were snakes, blind albino snakes slithering around me and evil rat eyes reflecting the light from my Bling as I puffed vapor out of my nose. It seemed all the toilets from some massive skyscraper were flushing upon me as the floor became steeper and I lost my balance and landed on my back and went down a water slide with the Bling lit in front of me, plowing feet first through the muck and rats and snakes and spider webs into a dark pit that I fell into, the sludge splashing down with me onto a circular grate that siphoned out the liquid but left much of the solids on me. "Uuugh," I moaned, drenched and shaking. I saw a rusty door with faded letters stenciled onto it that said Sears Tower SL 5 and I grabbed the little padlock that was binding it and to my surprise it broke apart in my hand, held together after forty-five years by nothing but rust, and so I bashed my shoulder against the door and it nudged open slightly. I bashed again and again until it creaked open wide enough for me to slip through.

I could only assume that I was in some sublevel of the Willis Tower (formerly known as the Sears Tower). Other than the door leading back out to the sewer, I was locked in a room with a single light bulb covered by a cage protruding from the ceiling. I couldn't go back the way I came, since my urine drenched Mega Bling had shorted out. As I was wondering how many years it would take for someone to find my skeletal remains, I discovered some old wooden crates, and choosing the sturdiest of them, I stacked them up and climbed. I used the top cap of my Genesis RBA to untwist the screws holding a grate to the ceiling and I pulled myself up and squirmed my way through some ductwork, inch by inch, until I came across the next grate that I managed to bash off with my elbow after no less than twenty attempts. I slid through, arms and head first, and fell down into an expansive area, landing to a dead stop on something made out of metal that had a gigantic dusty tarp over it. The object under the tarp was rounded like a cylinder, so I couldn't keep my balance and slid off of it to the floor, where I lie on my back breathing deeply in pain and confusion.

When I came to my senses, I attempted to rise by

grabbing the tarp to pull myself up but it slid and kept on sliding with the force of gravity down upon me, landing on me one fold after another. It was a huge, heavy tarp and I struggled to free myself from it as it suffocated me, finding an opening in what felt like seconds before death. I crawled out from under it, rolling once again on my back to catch my breath. I looked up at the object that had been hidden under the tarp. It was a missile. I'm not talking about some little backyard firework. I'm talking about a full-fledged missile with a warhead on it, the kind that can take out a full city block. It even had one of those orange and black symbols on it that looks like three blades of a fan.

"What is a missile doing in the Sears Tower?" I asked myself, because no Chicagoan calls it the Willis Tower, after all. I stumbled back, gazing at it. It had four fins and was on a trailer that had a tongue socket the size of a mush ball. As I fumbled away from its contagion, my ass crashed into what felt like a metal counter top and, reaching back to level myself, the palm of my hand depressed a bulbous button. The room lit up with twirling red lights that flashed around on the ceiling and an ear splitting horn honked then wailed then honked then wailed as a female, computerized voice coming from everywhere started counting down: *T-minus one twenty, t-minus one nineteen, t-minus one eighteen.* I cried out and hopped around like a mouse stuck in a box. There was an oblong metal door at the far end of the space, the top of which had wheels attached to a track, so I rushed to it and slid it open and in my haste I stepped through and fell down a full story, landing on a metal plate with thick cables attached to it. Below me, I heard voices shouting in desperation, "Move move move!!" as the computer voice kept counting down, *T-minus one-o-three, t-minus one-o-two* and I realized I was on top of an elevator as the voices below me gathered in it and I began to rise. The elevator stopped and someone shouted, "Good God! Delta protocol! Now!! I'm going in! Get up to the main floor and start the evacuation," and the sliding door was violently slammed shut and the elevator rose again at an ear popping speed and when it stopped whoever was inside went rushing away shouting into a squawking radio. The fire alarms blared and there was a voice over an intercom saying, *Delta protocol 1 9 5 this is not a drill. Delta Protocol 1 9 5 this is not a drill.* I slid the ceiling panel away and hopped into the elevator with a humph and calmly joined the rest of the people who were rushing toward the exits, escaping hurriedly, but not too panicky, looking as inconspicuous as a person in a trilby and trench coat splattered with human waste can look.

That was actually when I escaped out into the late afternoon sun, where a black sedan was squealing to a halt and men covered in hazmat suits were jogging so wobbly toward the tower it looked as if they would fall over. That was actually when I searched for my holographic cartomizer. I shook my head as I discovered it missing. I *thought* I had felt a rather odd tug while Elle and I were tangled under the tables of Vaporee.

Well, my long lost lover, the Sears Tower didn't blow up so they must have deactivated that missile in time, but as you can imagine, I was awfully paranoid after nearly nuking Chicago. Surely my slimy fingerprints would be found somewhere in that bunker under the skyscraper, so I was rather alarmed when I came home and was making my way up the back porch stairs to crawl through the hole in the attic and I saw Brandon's rock hard, dimpled buttocks pounding away between the legs of some curly haired blonde with veiny breasts like honeydews on the other side of the window. Brandon sensed my presence and shouted, "Mel!" I held my forehead and grimaced, as he leapt off the bed in the nude and approached me from the other side of the glass with his condom still clinging to his shrinking member.

"What's up BB?" I asked.

"Yo bro someone's here to see you."

"What?"

"Yeah bro some broad's up there," he said, pointing to the attic.

"Someone's up there?" I asked, bewildered. "In *my* room?"

Brandon slapped himself violently on the head. "Was that out of bounds, letting someone up there when you're not around?" he asked apologetically, his condom still clinging to him like a persistent blob of snot as he lost his erection. "Man, bro, what was I thinking? I should respect your space dog. Bro, man, dude, you know, like I've never, you know, had a, what do call it?"

"A tenant," I said.

"Right bro, I was going to say like a roomie, but you're more like a tenant," he shouted through the window pane.

"It's okay," I flustered. "I'll go check it out."

"Yo sho bro?"

"Sure," I said, glancing up at the trap suspiciously. "Go ahead and get back knee deep in it." The woman on his bed smiled and wiggled her fingers at me.

"My man," Brandon cheered as I started my ascent up the aluminum ladder.

I poked my head cautiously through the trap and looked into my cubbyhole, my eyes just above floor level. All three of the spiral light bulbs that were strung over supporting beams were lit, and someone had opened the tiny window that was a foot or two behind my head, as well as the window at the front, causing a breeze to run through that lifted the dust and caused it to float around in the harsh light like moving galaxies. As I shielded my eyes with my hand, I could see that someone was sitting on one of my kitchen chairs, could make out a pair of feet wearing oxfords made out of doily material and leather, with thick strings bow knotted like birthday presents and white socks up to the shins of stubbly legs. As my vision adjusted, I could make out a white lace dress that appeared like an apparition. I gained a firm footing on the plywood with my knees, and as I kneeled there using my hand as a visor, I called out, "Who's there?" Yugo, we're both adults, so I can admit to you I felt a bit aroused at the thought of being alone in my hiding place with some mysterious woman in her frilly lace outfit.

"Ah, there you are at last," she said, her voice dry and vibrating, like plucking a bass string.

"Who's that?" I inquired again, standing in the middle of the space so I didn't bang my head. I stepped forward, still struggling to correct my vision in the drab attic defiled by bare lights. She sat with a manila folder on her lap that she flipped open with a hand inside of a white glove.

"Melvin?" she asked. I could make out a thick, curly head of red hair as I approached.

"Maybe," I said. "What's this about?"

Her fingers pulled something out of her folder and she lifted it up for me to see. It was my business card. As my face passed one of the light bulbs, putting it behind me, she came into clear view. Any erotic notion I had about this strange encounter vanished like a soap bubble. She was quite frankly as homely as a blood hound, with a long nose pocked by alcoholism, her face overdone with thick lipstick and rouge and eyeliner like a painted china doll, her wig of curls completely unconvincing. One of her legs had graying purple bruises on it.

I was infuriated. "What the hell is this all about?" I shouted at her.

She was startled and fumbled the folder in her gloved hands, her fake eyelashes blinking rapidly; but she soon took a breath and maintained her composure like flipping a switch. "You're not exactly George Clooney, you know."

I instinctually pulled my trilby to the right to cover the burn scar that spreads like pink mesh from my temple to my ear.

"Who do you think you are, barging in here like this?" I growled.

"Excuse me?" she said with drastically rising inflection. "I assumed this was your office. I assumed meeting your clients here was standard." She lifted up my business card and shoved it toward my face.

"This address isn't even on that card!" I pointed out, flipping a finger at it.

"You came highly recommended," she insisted.

"Only a handful of people know about this place," I challenged. "Who recommended me?"

"I met her in a bar," she defended, adjusting her clothing with pinches from both her hands. "She said you did something for her, something involving" and her voice trembled and she stuttered rapidly like a laser sliding across a compact disk totaled by a scratch. "Ahahbaba-cacadada-fefegaga-jajakaka-lalamama." (I may have nodded slightly at this point.) "Mama? Momemie?"

"Mice?" I helped.

"Yes! Yes!" she said closing her eyes and nodding. "It was the job involving the mice. Her name was" and she shook her head, struggling to speak, but instead she began stuttering some more nonsense. "Zazayaya-wawavava-tatasasa" (I may have gestured impatiently for her to spit it out.) "Sasa?"

"Sandra!" I said for her.

"Yes! Yes! Sandra referred you," and she sighed greatly and relaxed in her chair, smiling at me.

Sandra had answered my "No Job Too Dirty" ad in the local shopper. She wanted revenge on her ex-lover, Peter, who had a horrible phobia regarding rodents. From what she told me, he would jump up on a chair and shriek like a woman whenever he saw one. Peter got fed up with the way Sandra constantly chewed her nails, and he broke the relationship off abruptly, without further explanation, standing her up on their next date. He refused to talk to her about it and even changed his phone number. In retaliation, Sandra went around to various pet shops and bought up their live mice, which she kept in a big plastic storage bin. There must have been a hundred of them in there, constantly hopping like so many jumping beans. She hired me to sneak into Peter's house and dump the mice in his basement, where they would most certainly work their way around, infesting his home to terrorize him. She even had a key to his back door so the job seemed easy enough. I borrowed a Toyota Camry from my Uncle Nick's lot (from his *secret* lot, the one where the vehicles are stripped of their VINs as they await disassembly) and I had a hard time maneuvering the container in and out of the car as all the mice shifted their collective weight around.

Peter's basement was a recreation center with an

air hockey table and a full bar, and I thought that was an awful shame, but I was being paid, so I unsnapped the container lid and as a dozen mice jumped up at my hand, I squealed and flung it away from me. Mice flew all over the place. Up until that point, I forgot that I didn't much like rodents either. As they scampered at my feet I dashed around trying to avoid them, stepping on a few of them in my mad rush back up the basement stairs, during which the Vapor Shark DNA in my trench coat pocket must have gotten whacked just perfectly by the hand rail, a freak accident that rendered the screen at its bottom useless. I got out of there and was paid a hundred and fifty dollars, not even enough to cover my damaged box mod.

I pulled up the other kitchen chair and sat on it, still red in the face. "Well you shouldn't go around startling people like that," I complained. "You could call and make an appointment."

She shrugged her broad shoulders and stuck her lower lip out. "The number on this card seems to be out of order."

"My minutes must have expired," I said, shifting in my seat and adjusting my trilby. "Thanks for letting me know" and I cleared my throat. "I'll get right on that."

"Vera," she said, hunching forward and offering me her hand. "Vera Grimmel."

She had one of those handshakes that I hate—the kind that makes every attempt not to make contact and instead just hovers there cupped like a shell. I felt the urge to take my handshake back.

"Miss Grimmel, it's been a long weekend. If you don't mind, get to the point."

I wasn't lying. I had had a long, screwed up weekend. As a matter of fact, I had just come from Granmama's house.

Late last spring, Granmama decided she no longer needed to wear her clothes. She was detained by police twice: once for boarding a bus in the buff and once for running a red light wearing only a smile. We were afraid she was coming down with Alzheimer's but her doctor brushed it off as Senior Rebellion and gave her a prescription for medical marijuana. It was agreed upon between my sister Alice, my brother Porphy and Uncle Nick that we would take turns checking in on her at the house in Oriole Park. Porphy soon excused himself by accepting a job with a military contractor hired to conduct covert missions in Syria. Alice simply did not have the stomach to endure Granmama unbathed and in a confused state of mind. She ended up having nervous breakdowns that only made matters worse. She did the best she could, which was to adopt Halo so that Granmama wouldn't keep using dog walking as an excuse to streak through the neighborhood. And Uncle Nick, well Uncle Nick was Uncle Nick. He may be able to sell a blind man a used car, but getting his mother into the tub to give her a sponge bath, let's just say it wasn't going to happen. So it ended up being me who checked in on Granmama, and that involved quite a subway ride. When I did manage to get all the way out there, I would find her wading in filth but seldom in poor spirits. If you'll excuse the clichés, she may have decided to go through her twilight years as batty as a belfry but at least she was as happy as a camper.

A couple of weeks before meeting Vera Grimmel, I found Granmama in her back yard tending her garden on her hands and knees completely in the raw, her body black with filth, potting soil lodged between her buttocks from squatting and digging. I got her inside and into the tub, where she played with her rubber ducky and slapped her hands against the bubbles. Her naked gardening was becoming a habit that I simply could not talk her out of.

"Why are you doing that?" I pleaded.

"I've nothing left to do. Nobody comes to visit me anymore. I've even been fired from the forum," she explained as I rubbed her back with a bar of soap.

For a few months Granmama had been hired by vape-mania.com as a forum moderator in exchange for free vaping supplies. "Vape Mania fired you?" I asked.

"They *let me go*," she cried. "Now I don't have anything to vape."

"What about your Janeiro?" I asked.

"I took the plastic bottle out of the box to clean it, and now I can't find it."

"All you need is a new bottle," I assured her.

"Oh," she said and frowned. "I guess I shouldn't have thrown it out then."

"If I get you something nice, will you just sit on the back porch and have a vape and not undress in your garden?"

She grabbed my bicep with both her wet hands and yanked at me, her eyes going bright. "Yes! Yes!" she said in an excited way, and she closed her eyes and clenched her false teeth and then spit it out. "I want a Gold Plated Variable Voltage Volarie YingYang with Digital Display!"

"What?" I laughed, but she peered at me nodding her head up and down like a child wanting a pony. I was taken aback. I was thinking of going down to ZestyD's Vape Shop and getting her a cheap Evod kit, but she blurted out one of the most coveted and might I say expensive mods on the market. "Okay, Granmama, I'll see what I can do."

I instantly regretted saying that. I felt guilty for getting her hopes up. Not only would a YingYang run about $400 but it didn't even matter. Every time I went to the library and checked online, Vo-Vape was completely sold out of that particular mod; it was a custom made item with preorders stacked up, and whenever it did become available it was sold out again within minutes by those who had signed up for email alerts. I spent countless hours in the Vape Mania website, the e-cigarette forum that the book with my moniker on it was titled after, refreshing the screen over and over, hoping that someone would offer a YingYang for sale but it never happened.

Searching around for it some more, I stumbled across a YouTube video from Bill Picardo. Are you familiar with Bill? Bill has made a real name for himself in the vaping community. He's quite the celebrity, *thee* best known vaping product critic in the universe, his video reviews receiving tens of thousands of hits. All his videos begin with the sound of thunder clapping as a godlike voice commands, *Vape the Juice!!* Bill is a likeable guy with a plump, tan face and a deep, soothing voice who keeps his reviews simple and who isn't arrogant and that's probably his attraction. He's a slightly chubby man who uses a lot of hand gestures; and his graying hair is always kept neatly combed back and he sports a goatee that he most likely trims himself. He really knows his vaping stuff and can go on for hours talking about the pros and cons of various vaping gear and juices. I stuck the earpiece in so I wouldn't disturb the library as I watched his video review of the Gold Plated YingYang from Vo-Vape.

"Hey folks. BPicardo here. You know, the Volarie is one of those devices that's been around for a long time," and he shoved a sparkling gold canister into my face, like the housing of a fancy medium sized flashlight clenched in his fist, "and it has a huuuuge fan base. Let's just say if you were to post something negative about the Volarie at Vape Mania or at some other forum, well, Volarie fans would sense it with their Volarie radar like vampire bats to mosquitoes and they would appear in droves seemingly out of nowhere and most likely threaten to suck your children's blood as they vigorously defend their favorite PV." He stopped to have a vape from his Volarie, blowing a thick white cloud out of his nostrils like a dragon. "You may have witnessed this and so you went to the Vo-Vape website to see what it's all about and you're probably still nursing your sore jaw that dropped to the floor when you saw the prices. Well I have one now," he said, waving the gold YingYang at me as if it was a magic wand, "and I have held it, and I have vaped from it, and all I can say is NOW I GET IT."

I had a huge Steampunk mod in my pocket and adjusted myself accordingly. Wink wink.

"All right, what I have here is the Gold Plated Volarie YingYang. It has a 3.5 amp switch which means you're going to be able to push some additional power to your lower resistance atomizers without shorting it out. It holds two 18650 batteries and let me tell you, it's heavy," and he dangled it for me to see, as a bit of drool collected on my lower lip. "This baby is built solid, a quality PV. The threads on here are smooth like mushroom soup. The connector on here is 510 and it has a nice big drip well around it. The top cap matches the bottom battery cap; both have this fancy Asian style etching that just looks fantastic and there are ridges in the middle," he said, holding up the canister and pointing at it with his thick index finger, "to help your grip. The button is where I like a button to be, closer to the top of the mod. It sticks out so you can find it with no fumbling. And obviously you have the screen for your settings. The gold finish is satiny so the grip is really solid on these." He paused his review to have another vape, blowing a cloud at me. He gave a little moan and then continued. "This Volarie is a variable voltage device. Let's talk about the user interface . . ."

And Bill Picardo went on and on demonstrating how to use the device's button to change the voltage or to check the ohms or to check the strength of your batteries and so on. "I have to give the YingYang a score of ten out of ten as well as an owl hoot," Bill concluded. An animated owl popped up and went *Hoot hoot!* "In fact, I like this mod so much, this is what I'll be taking with me to the Vaporee Vaping Festival in Chicago next weekend."

Someone sat next to me and spoke. I turned to look. It was a hipster white boy with dreadlocks, sitting at the next computer, his chair turned completely toward me as he talked to me. I took the earpiece out. "I'm sorry, what?"

"That's some fedora you have there," he said.

I shook my head in contempt. "This is a trilby, not a fedora. A trilby is a completely different hat."

"Oh yeah?"

"Yeah. It has a narrower brim. I don't know why everyone thinks this is a fedora. I specifically wrote that I wore a trilby but those jerks who edited the book changed it to a fedora. They probably assumed people are too stupid to know what a trilby is."

"You wrote a book?" he asked.

"It's more like a memoir, well, really, more like a private diary. It was in my storage unit when the contents were auctioned off. So they say they own it because they bought it at auction. Well we'll see about that."

"Seriously?"

"Absolutely. And the style of my hat wasn't the only thing they changed. They added a bunch of creepy stuff and plugged in all sorts of product placements. I'm embarrassed to have my name on it."

"I couldn't help but notice that you're watching BPicardo," the hipster said.

"Yeah, so?"

"Well," he said, easing his backpack up between his legs and slowly unzipping it. "You're him. You're Melvin Provario."

I was shocked. "What makes you say that?"

"Oh come on. The overcoat? And the fedora?"

"It's a trench coat. And a trilby!" I shouted and people in the library started shushing me.

"You were just babbling about your book. My name's Mike Crow and I work for VMZ."

"The Vaporazzi?"

"I prefer the term Vaporigative Journalist." He started sliding his camera out of his backpack.

"Don't do that," I said, reaching forward and shoving his camera back down into the bag.

"Hey, don't touch my camera," he complained.

"Why do you want to take my picture?" I insisted.

"What kind of question is that?" he laughed. "You're the man responsible for the Vaporgate scandal." He struggled to pull his camera up as I placed both my hands on it and shoved it back down. "Cut it out!" he complained, attempting to keep his voice down in the library. "What the hell do you think you're doing?"

"I'll show you what I'm doing," I said and I clutched his backpack and yanked it off his lap and tossed it. It hit the floor and rolled away. Before he could finish whatever verbal complaint was about to come out of his mouth, I leapt up and began retrieving books from a shelf, flinging them at him as if they were Frisbees. They struck and bounced off him as he attempted to dodge them, protecting his face with his arms and lifting one of his legs in an attempt to block his torso.

"What're you, off your meds again? Cut it out!" Mike laughed but he quickly became more serious and angry. "Stop it I said!"

"Sir!" the librarian shouted. "Please leave the premises or I'm calling the police."

I darted out of the library and jumped onto the back of an old pick-up truck that had a clothes drier bungeed to its bed and I hung on, balancing on the bumper, clinging to the tailgate as the light turned green and the truck drove away blasting what I assumed was Mexican music out of the cab; but it wasn't—it was a live medley of polka hits.

Apples peaches pumpkin pie
Who's not ready holler I
Let's all play hide and seek

I turned back and gave Mike Crow the middle finger as he came rushing out of the library after me; and I rode on the back of the truck like that for several blocks, singing along to the polka at the top of my lungs.

Rosie's my baby!!
I don't mean maybe!!
She is my sweetie pie!!

And that brings me back to Vaporee. You see, my dear, it's true that I escaped from the Willis Tower into the late afternoon sun, but actually that wasn't the end of it. I fully intended to make my way east to hop on an el train but who do you think I saw entering the hotel as the men in hazmat suits were wobbling by? It was Bill Picardo. In the flesh. He was shorter than I imagined him to be but it was definitely him; there was no mistaking that tan, round face if his. I followed him down a series of escalators into the vaping festival, keeping my distance. People recognized him and he was very gracious, stopping to shake hands and share a few words and have a good laugh. I kept my trilby over my brow and maneuvered through the crowd until I got to the table that earlier I had been hiding under. I stood there for a while making *psssst* sounds but got no response, so I crouched down as if tying my shoe and lifted the drape, but Elle was no longer there. I kept one eye on Bill Picardo's movement as my other eye scanned the room for Elle, who I soon found sitting in the food court eating some cheese fries. I sat across from her at her table.

She waved her hand in front of her face and said, "Whew! Juniper. What happened to you?"

"Long story," I said and I lowered my voice. "Listen, I know you stole my holographic carto." She was about to protest but I interrupted. "That's okay, keep it. But I need your help. You see that guy over there," and I nonchalantly pointed.

"Who? Picardo?" she asked, mystified by my discretion.

"Yeah. He's a famous vaping critic."

"Yeah, duh."

"I have it from good authority that he's carrying a Gold Plated Volarie YingYang on him. Do you think you can, you know, do that little thing you do?"

"Why would I want to do that?" she demanded, surprised by my straightforwardness.

"For my Granmama," I said.

"I don't know, man. This is odd."

"Well if you don't think you can pull it off—"

She pressed her lips together, peering at me

through thin slits. "If I get that Volarie, you're going to owe me big time," she said.

"Yes, of course."

"I mean, like for the rest of your life, Melvin!"

"Assuming you can pull it off," I tempted.

"Okay, okay, I can see that you're challenging me," she said, nodding her head. She stood up mechanically and walked toward Picardo who was now in the middle of the exhibit hall basking in his notoriety as humbly as possible. Elle browsed some tables making her way toward him and then feigned surprise at seeing him. She shook his hand and had a conversation with him, patting him playfully and insisting on shaking his hand again and again; she tickled his ribs and he was enjoying the exchange. When Elle came back to the table she sat down and said, "Sorry, he wasn't carrying a Volarie. He had an SVR but no Volarie."

"That doesn't make sense," I complained. "He himself said he was bringing his Volarie to Vaporee."

"Maybe he's charging his batteries," Elle said with a shrug.

"Rats," I moaned. "How am I going to break this to Granmama?"

"Just hold on there, Skippy. Maybe he's charging his batteries *in his hotel room*."

"So you think he's staying in this hotel?" I asked.

"Where else would he stay? At some *other* hotel? Besides," and she offered a mischievous smile and held out the palm of her hand. She had the keycard to his room.

"Holy macaroni," I blurted, impressed beyond measure.

"Shall we?" she offered.

"What? Now?" I asked, caught off guard.

"Sure," she said. "We know he's not in his room,

so what better time to have a look and see. Maybe we'll find that YingYang of yours."

So, my dear Yugo, that's what we did. We went up the escalators and Elle went to the reception desk and simply asked what room her Uncle Picardo was in and it was room 910. We took the elevator to the ninth floor, making jokes about how the hallway looked like the one from The Shining and how we expected it to be flooded with blood at any moment. The joke took an unexpected turn when two little girls wearing blue dresses came walking hand in hand toward us and skipped away into the vending room. We laughed and held our mouths in unison, jinxing each other. When we found the room we stood outside, building up nerve, giggling and saying, "Yeah? Yeah? Yeah?" to each other until we both said, "Yeah!" and she slid the card through. The light blinked green and we slipped on in. It was a nice two room unit, with a parlor of sorts with a television and two lamps on end tables at either side of a couch with some abstract art on the walls. We could see the foot of a bed in the adjacent room through a slightly opened door. And I saw it, the YingYang, gold and shining like a holy relic, standing on the farthest end table next to a plastic charger with two batteries in it.

Elle became extremely nervous all of a sudden. "Just get it and let's get out of here," she insisted.

I went rushing toward the YingYang but the sound of a baby crying came from the bedroom and we heard a toilet flush. We jinxed each other again, saying, "Oh crap!" and I took Elle by her arm and pulled her into a closet, folding the louver doors shut. We watched through the horizontal slates as Mrs. Picardo came out of the bedroom carrying a child in a diaper. She was wearing a gray sweatshirt sporting an emblem, a shield with two cutlasses crossing with a pirate's skull-face, and there was a mini version of this emblem on the ass of her sweatpants as well. Mrs. Picardo sat down on the couch, bouncing her baby in her arm; she picked up the remote control, pointed it and clicked and was delighted to discover a subtitled version of Laagan beginning. I don't know if you've ever seen it, but if not, it's a four hour musical about a game of cricket. She pulled up her sweatshirt and began breastfeeding as we hid from her a few feet away.

After a while, Elle sat cross legged on the floor and played Angry Birds on her phone with the sound off. I was getting a crick in my neck avoiding the coat pole so I slid down the wall and settled in the corner and nodded in and out of sleep. Finally I was relieved to hear Mrs. Picardo yawn greatly after the evil Brits were beaten by the loving Hindus, and she turned the television off and went into the bedroom with her child, closing the door behind her. I woke Elle who was out like a light and we opened the closet door and I crept toward the YingYang, but a horrible pounding startled us and we dashed back into our hiding place. "Honey I'm locked out!" shouted Bill and Mrs. Picardo came out of the bedroom walking in her sleep to let him in and she immediately went back to the bedroom and shut the door. Bill sat down on the couch and set up a video camera on a little tripod and set up a laptop next to it and connected everything together with wires and then he put the batteries in his YingYang and attached a drip atomizer to it and he began speaking to the camera.

"BPicardo here and I'm at the Vaporee Vaping Festival and look what I have," and he held out a glass bottle with a rubber bulb on it. "That's right, today we'll be taking a look at Stratagem. How can I describe this apple pie, cinnamony flavor with just a touch of French vanilla," and he paused to make noises with his mouth. "Ma ma, ba ba, ka ka, mamamama," and he did a series of exercises with his lips and tongue. "Let's have a vape, quaa quaa quaa, let's have a vape, mooo mooo mooo, let's have a vape." Not yet satisfied with himself, he untied his shoes and pulled them off and plopped his feet up on the glass table and wiggled his toes within his brown socks and he had a few big vapes and then he sat up and started again. "BPicardo here and I'm at the Vaporee Vaping Festival and look at what I have here," and he proceeded to talk about the Stratagem juice while he dripped it and vaped it, stopping and resaying things in slightly different ways, in slightly different order, with slightly different tones, pausing the camera and adjusting it to film at different angles, and he did this for the next two hours as we sat behind the closet door with our heads in our hands, watching him through the slates. Elle nudged me and I read her lips as she silently mouthed, *It's midnight.* At first I didn't grasp the significance of this, but then it dawned upon me. *Happy birthday*, I mouthed back and she smiled and I put my hand on the back of her head and drew her near me and we kissed. I put my arms around her and we kissed some more and just as the heat was making me wonder how we could possibly pull it off in that cramped space, we heard Bill snoring.

He had fallen back with his arms spread over the back of the couch, with his feet propped up, and he was snoring like a motorboat. His YingYang was still in his hand. We crept out of the closet and tiptoed to him and I skillfully pinched the YingYang and ever so gently lifted it with a twist out of his dead grip, and I snatched the bottle of Stratagem, as well as the battery charger; and Elle to my horror managed to get his wallet out of

44

his pants and she pilfered the money out of it and then slipped it back in, and I shook my head vehemently in objection but she ignored me as she got his watch off his wrist, and I nearly had a heart attack as she slipped the leather belt off his waist, and then she pulled his socks off his feet and I have no idea what she was going for next as she hunched over the snoring man but I stood firm and pulled her away and there was a silent struggle in which we gave each other faces until she reluctantly surrendered. We tiptoed out of the hotel room with his stuff and casually walked to the elevator, went down to the lobby and escaped out into a less vibrant, nighttime Chicago.

"Why did you have to steal his socks?" I asked, befuddled.

"Why did you have to steal his YingYang?" she humphed back. "I'm sure if given the choice between his socks and his YingYang he'd prefer to have his YingYang," and then she stuck her fingers in her mouth and whistled loudly and a taxi pulled up and she hopped in the back of it and shouted to me, "See you on the flip side, Melvin Profarttio," and the taxi dashed away.

The next day I was on my way to the train station to surprise Granmama with her new mod when it just so happened I was passing the Balance Vape Den. I saw through the window that two dweebs were sitting at the bar vaping away. I only discovered the Vape Den a week or so before; it had simply appeared out of nowhere on Halsted in Bridgeport, so I wandered in to check it out and found those same two dweebs vaping at the bar. At first I thought it was a dweeb and a chick but upon closer observation, it was just two dweebs. There was also some Mexican pseudo-biker type (you know, a guy who dresses like a biker but doesn't actually own a bike) with tattoos all over his arms talking to a young Asian guy behind the bar. I took a seat. The pseudo-biker was sampling various juice flavors from Protank Minis that the vapetender offered him with brief descriptions, such as, *This one is a Jolly Rancher with some menthol undertones.* I sat there for ten full minutes, and not a single person in the room acknowledged my existence. Finally, I said to one of the dweebs, "Those are *some* clouds you're blowing," and admittedly they were, so thick and white they almost seemed to be solid, but the dweeb only smiled without looking at me and showed off some more.

"So how much do those bottles cost?" I asked the vapetender as he produced another sample for the Mexican, who kept saying, *Mmm, that one's good too. I'll take one of those.* I received no answer. I sat there like a fool, as if completely invisible to those doofus hipsters. Me, Melvin Provario, the man who quite literally wrote the book on vaping, was being treated as if I wasn't hip enough to vape with. "Okay, I guess I'll come by some other time," I stuttered in embarrassment as I left.

Of course I intended to *never* come back, but then I saw an opportunity for a bit of revenge. That day I was fully armed with a Gold Plated Volarie YingYang connected to Bill's badass drip atomizer that was producing bigger clouds than my lungs had ever before endured. I would walk right in there and fire up my coveted variable voltage mod and blow a cloud of Stratagem, no less, one of the most expensive juices out there, right into the faces of those dweebs. I walked in but for reasons I can't explain, I had butterflies in my stomach and my heart was palpitating and my knees felt wobbly and I fumbled into my trench coat with a trembling hand that betrayed me; and before I could get my mod out, I noticed that the little dweeb was sitting there vaping off an identical Gold Plated YingYang. My mouth hung open as he ignored me and blasted a thick white ball out of his mouth like a massive male ejaculation into crystal clear water.

"Can I help you with something?" the vapetender asked as if I was someone who was lost and looking for directions.

"Why you little twat!" I shouted at the dweeb.

The twat looked at me with surprise; he summed me up from head to foot. "Hey Hershel," he said. "The 1940s called. It wants its clothes back."

Everyone was laughing as I stormed out of the place; but of course the joke was on them, because how long did they really expect to stay in business with nothing but the same two dweebs as customers?

When I got to Granmama's I found her trying to bake a bowl of Jell-O in the oven. As I stood with her in her kitchen washing her dishes for her, I noticed there was a green leaf sticking out of the elastic at the back of her pants. "Okay Granmama, let me have a look," and I poked my finger under the elastic and pulled it away, discovering a thin green twig with leaves on it stuck between her buttocks. "Granmama, you were working nude in the garden again, weren't you?"

"No, I don't think so," she said.

"Yes you were. And you were there cleaning the seeds out your weed too. I know."

"How do you know? You've been spying on me?"

"No, I haven't been spying on you. But you dropped a seed between your legs and now you have a marijuana plant growing out of your ass."

"Oh Deary," she said.

"Come on, let's take care of this," I said and helped her into her bathroom. I had her stand in the tub and I pulled down her slacks and sure enough there was a marijuana plant growing out of a clod of mud that was jammed between her buttocks. As I tried to pull it free, it seemed the root had worked its way into her anus. "Oh Granmama," I whined, "I think we should get you to the hospital."

"No, no hospital. No doctors. They'll lock me up."

"Okay, then, but if I pull anything important out of you, you can't blame me." I went to her medicine cabinet and dabbed some petroleum jelly on my finger and then held my breath and plunged my finger into her anus, rotating it to make sure I lubricated it well; and then I pulled on the plant and it slid out nicely. I gave her a shower and got her dressed and we sat on her back porch not mentioning what had just happened.

"Oh, I almost forgot," I said and rummaged through my trench coat to find the YingYang.

Her eyes lit up. "Oh Deary. Look at that! Will you look at that!"

"It's for you" I said with a satisfied smile.

"For me? Ooooh," and she kissed me on the cheek.

"Now you promised. No more gardening in the nude, okay?"

"Okay, I promise," she said and she took a vape off the atomizer. "Oooh, that's good." I put the bottle of Stratagem on her palm and closed her hand around it.

"Take this, enjoy."

So as you can see, after finally getting home to relax after *that* weekend, I was in no mood to take any shit from some strange lady in my own private crawlspace. "Come out with it," I said to Vera Grimmel. "What do you want?"

Here is where my letter must end, for now, my Dear Yugo. As you can see, my fingerprints are messing up the pages. I have a job playing Woody the Clown for a group of Girl Scout Daisies and I've been putting on my makeup. I will write again soon. Until then—

XOXO,
Your Dear Melvin

Exhibit 15

Drawing on piece of paper.
Found in the attic of Dexter and Wang Bieberman.

SECOND WRAP: Five Pawns

Dear Yugo,

When last I wrote I wanted to confess to you the things I had done, but as you know I went off on some tangents. The pining I feel when I recall our brief time together is distracting and it pains me to think that coming clean may put more distance between us. But if we are to have a life together, it will have to be based on mutual honesty and trust, so with this second letter I will keep to the point. Please forgive that I am not including a return address nor am I attempting to contact you by means other than these letters. First give me the chance to explain completely and then make up your mind. If you will have nothing to do with me, then it is better that you aren't burdened with my exact whereabouts, as it may be pried out of you; but if you decide, as I hope with all my heart that you will, that we are meant to be soul mates, in that case I will give a little clue at the end of my correspondence that only you will be able to decipher.

Sometimes we must open old wounds to flush out the infection. I must offer a belated apology for how we abruptly parted ways. This should have been the first thing I said to you. You were completely unresponsive that morning, and I have no other excuse but that I panicked. I am sure your cataleptic behavior was due to epilepsy or perhaps narcolepsy or some other natural infliction that you are haunted with; we all have our flaws. But that morning, in my half-awake stupor and under the spell of our shared carnal experience, I saw an Amber Alert online with the photo of a girl who to my fuzzy eyes looked a bit like you. In passing, it dawned upon me that of course it couldn't have been you, but at the time I thought it would be in our mutual interests if we unconnected the dots between us. Oh how I wish you were conscious in back of the bicycle rickshaw that I borrowed, as I raced toward Hollywood Beach, because it was a beautiful, romantic sunrise over the lake. I'm sorry you missed it.

When I killed Bartholomew Zigfield, I was completely composed and my conscience was clear. As I've admitted to you, I had a panic attack when I went into the Balance Vape Den to show off my Volarie, so why do I react so irrationally in one instance (as I did with you on that morning) but with such a clear head in more dire circumstances? I could say that it is simply a matter of caring but I've come to accept it's more inexplicable than that. It is as if there are two of me living in one body. I fondly remember when we were in my room shot gunning vapor and I offered to give your body an examination; in jest you called me Doctor Melvin. If that part of me that you love so well is Doctor Melvin, then let's call the other part that lives inside of me Mr. Vape.

Mr. Vape entered Bart Zigfield's room wearing a white coat that he borrowed from a closet that he found himself trapped in for an hour during his infiltration of the hospital. Bart was on the bed, covered to his chest with a sheet and blanket, his arms penetrated by a web of tubes leading to IV bags as if he was a balloon salesman. Bart's head looked like an egg with eyes, so stripped of hair by chemotherapy and absent of expression it was. Mr. Vape walked to his bedside and checked the man's chart. "Bartholomew Zigfield," he read out loud. He leaned over the body and inspected the man's hand. "Nice tattoo," he said, gently tracing the Z in it with the tip of his finger. As the man's brown eyes bulged and rolled toward Mr. Vape, he came out and asked him: "Bart? Is that you?"

"Yes," the patient said like a deflating tire, then like some ominous bird in the night, he said, "Who are you?"

"The angel of vape," Mr. Vape whispered. He reached under his white coat into the pocket of his trench coat and retrieved a plastic squeeze bottle that was once a ketchup bottle from the table of a diner. Inside the bottle was a thin solution containing 10,000 milligrams of nicotine. "The initial symptoms of nicotine poisoning are similar to an amphetamine overdose," Mr. Vape explained. "You'll experience salivation, sweating, nausea and abdominal pain. Then your heart rate will speed up and you'll lose coordination, followed by headache, dizziness, tremors, muscle spasms and seizures," he continued.

"What?" Bart sobbed with floury, trembling lips.

"I'll sit here with you through the stimulatory phase as you enter the second phase of nicotine poisoning. You see, nicotine is both a stimulant *and* a depressant. So what you will experience next will be more like a barbiturate overdose. Your heart rate will begin to slow and you will have difficulty breathing; your central nervous system will become depressed and you will eventually become paralyzed; finally, you will fall into a coma and experience complete respiratory failure."

Bart weakly reached across his body toward the night stand next to his bed.

"Looking for this?" Mr. Vape asked, producing the nurse call button.

Bart's eyes bulged farther as his hand plopped down onto his chest.

"My guess is that upon your passing, there won't be any autopsy since you're in your final stages of terminal cancer. The problem is, Bart, you've been in your final stages of cancer for so very, very long. When did you plan on dying anyway?"

Bart sucked in two lungs of air and just as he was about to attempt his best effort at a cry for help, Mr. Vape jammed the point of the bottle into Bart's mouth. He took the bottle into both his hands and jammed it as far down Bart's throat as it would go, and he squeezed, leaning forward to put his lips to Bart's ear. "Taste my juice." Once the bottle was deflated, flat and empty, Mr. Vape put one hand on Bart's forehead and used the other to yank the bottle out. Bart made another attempt at shouting but he could only gurgle and cough. "Shhhhh," Mr. Vape exhaled with his finger over his lips, and he sat on a chair close to Bart and waited with him while the body jittered with spasms.

Mr. Vape took out his Aerotank and put his lips to it, sucking in a soothing menthol watermelon vapor and blowing it out like taking the lid off a pot of boiling soup. The vapor made his lungs feel cool and numb and he nodded off for just a second as the nicotine rushed to his head. The vapor was thick and white and lingered in the air much longer than he thought it would, making the room smell like cotton candy, as he waited for the machines to indicate problems with the patient's heart and respiration. As the machines began beeping like urgent alarms, Mr. Vape slipped out of the room, taking the long way around the hospital to the elevator, so that he wouldn't pass the nurses who were rushing from the desk to check on the dying patient.

Seems my mind is wandering all over the place like a scatterbrain again. I was telling you about the day I came home to find Vera Grimmel in the attic. I had become hostile and demanded to know what her game was, and seeing that she was prepared to talk, I sat on the kitchen chair and listened to her, the vapor from my PV collecting under the brim of my trilby.

"This past year," Vera said, her voice buzzing as if she had a dying bumblebee in her throat, "I've suffered great loss. First my little brother died and now more recently my father. My father passed away after a slow, agonizing struggle with emphysema, but my brother Patty's life was cut short, after he was bullied and tormented and tortured and murdered by a gang of ruffians. My brother looked a lot like that hero, uh, you know that *hero*" and Vera attempted to snap her gloved fingers together with no success as she began stuttering nonsensical gurgling noises. "Kakalala-manamana-parasa—"

"Yeah?" I encouraged her impatiently.

"Sasba-skasda-snasna—"

"Yeah?" I repeated twirling my hand.

"Snasne? Snisno? Snosno?"

"Oh for Pete's sake, are you trying to say Snowden?"

"Yes! Yes!" she panted, placing her spread fingers over her chest and catching her breath. "That's exactly who he looked like. Snowden!"

"What's wrong with you anyway?"

"Nervous stammer. S-s-sometimes I j-j-just can't get the words out."

"So your brother looked like Snowden," I said, impatiently gesturing for her to continue.

"Except he had red hair like mine," she said, flipping the back of her hand against the side of her dime store wig, "and his eyes were green and he was, how to put it mildly," and she whispered, "slightly, slightly, slightly—"

"Retarded?" I asked.

"Yes, that's right, retarded." The image of Patty in

55

my mind looked nothing like Snowden so I scowled at her. "Oh, but he held a lot of similar beliefs, was against spying and things like that," she maintained excitedly. "I can see that you sympathize with Snowden?"

"I agree with your brother, if that's what you're getting at."

"You see, Patty fell in with the wrong crowd. He was manipulated and tricked into thinking he was in debt to a group of racketeers. These racketeers, they peddle illegal cigarettes, have inside men working for Big Tobacco who pilfer the product in bulk. They have the machinery to roll them and package them. They print up phony name brand labels and sell them as authentic through a string of Snake Eyes convenience stores. They're nicknamed the Ziggies because the gang is run by the five Zigfield brothers."

She opened her manila folder and began producing sheets of paper, each with a photo of a man on it along with a few paragraphs of personal information. She set the papers on a milk crate that I produced for her.

"This is Larry Zigfield, age 37. He runs a liquor store on Lawrence Avenue called Ziggy Light's. He always wears those big bushy sideburns and those enormous black glasses. Very easy to spot. After a truckload of loose tobacco is hijacked, the contraband is taken to the space in the back of his store, where it sits for a while until the heat is off.

"Sooner or later the goods are taken to Red's Tobacco Shop in Logan Square, run by Roger Zigfield, age 39, otherwise known as Red. As you can see he has some discoloration like giant freckles on his cheeks. In the basement of his shop, the tobacco is rolled and packaged for distribution.

"This is Daniel Zigfield. At age 29, he's the

youngest of the crew. As you can see, he's a real work of art. A wigger with so much ink on his face, you can barely find his nose. He's presently living in Joliet, setting up a connection that will supply all the western suburbs with the ziggy cigs.

"Next we have Bartholomew, age 33. He was the muscle who went around convincing franchise owners that it would be in their best interest to mix some ziggy counterfeits in with their high volume of cigarette sales. Right now, though, he's in a hospice dying of cancer, so he may not be anything to worry about.

"Here's the ringleader. His name is Phil Zigfield but he goes by the nickname Smokey. He's 57. Rumor is his own mother recognized the devil in him and tried to kill him when he was a child and that's where that big scar that runs across his face came from. The story goes that rather than risk having another child in the house with her monster son, she waited until Phil was eighteen years old before she gave birth again. He runs a place called Smokey's Tavern near the corner of Paulina and Lunt. From the outside it appears to be just another neighborhood bar, but nobody from *that* neighborhood goes to it, and if you stepped in on any given night you'd find out why. It's a cesspool, a gathering place for the sleaziest and most corrupt and evil characters in Chicago.

"They have a backroom there, with a thick table with the Ziggy logo etched into it." I lowered my brow inquisitively. "Oh, the Ziggy logo is a design. There's a Z, and running through it vertically is a cigarette. It looks like an inverted dollar sign. Here, let me show you," and she poked her dry, cracked tongue with the tip of a thin felt marker and scrawled a sloppy version of the logo on a piece of paper for me. "It's in that backroom where the Ziggies hold their meetings, where

Phil bangs a gavel when it's decided someone needs to get smoked."

"How do you know all of this?" I asked.

"I have an *Inside Man*. All the Zigfields have the logo tattooed on their left hand, right here," and she pointed with her white glove, "on the webbing between the thumb and index finger. It's the same logo, the image of a Z with the burning cigarette crossing through it."

"Hold on a second," I said. "Do the police know about this?"

"The Ziggies have some connection, some institute of some sort, that *promotes* the use of cigarettes. I know that sounds ridiculous but it's true."

"I know it," I said, filling with disdain. "It's called IPIC."

"Under the umbrella of IPIC, the Ziggies have a pipeline to all levels of government. So the police?" She grimaced widely and I could see a smear of lipstick on her front tooth. "The police are easy to pay off. In fact, complaints to the police have been made in vain against the Ziggies, about instances of intimidation, regarding some of these alternative smoke shops that have been popping up. You know what I mean?" and she gestured toward the PV that I was vaping from.

"What sort of intimidation?" I asked.

"Well they want these smoke shops—"

"Vape shops," I corrected.

"—vape shops to sell their ziggies and when they refuse there are threats, and vandalism, and sometimes the city comes and shuts them down for no good reason."

"That's pretty lousy," I agreed.

"Not as lousy as what they did to my brother Patty."

"Okay I get it. You think these bastards killed your brother. I feel for you. I don't know what Sandra told you—but my dirty deeds *don't* come dirt cheap. I stick my neck out for nobody, and I'm not doing anyone any favors."

"I'm talking about money, Mr. Provario," she said, rubbing together the cloth over her thumb and two fingers. "My father was extremely wealthy. When my brother died, that should have left me the sole beneficiary. But Dad rewrote his will to stipulate that his money should be used first and foremost to bring the culprits who killed Patty to justice. He suggested a slew of specific, very expensive private investigators and lawyers to get the job done. Only after each and every last living Zigfield brother is behind bars for what they did to Patty, only then will I inherit whatever scraps are left."

"That's a raw deal, lady, but let me be frank. If you think I can get that job done any cheaper, with my limited experience and resources—if you think that somehow I can beat to the punch these professionals that your father has hired postmortem, and resolve this matter for you the cheapest way possible, you're deluding yourself. I don't have the first clue about how to convict these guys."

"I don't want convictions," Vera said.

"Well, what then?"

"Mr. Provario. I want you to kill them."

I laughed so loud that I caused Brandon and the broad he was with below to stir around on the squeaking bed.

"Please, it makes perfect sense," she said as I shook my head, rolling my eyes in disbelief. "The stipulation in the will says that every last *living* brother needs to be brought to justice, before any money is divvied out.

Every last *living* brother."

"Okay, first of all, you are clearly out of your mind. But let's just say, for the sake of argument, just to amuse you; let's just say that someone did take you up on your offer. I'm no fool. I know a little bit about litigation. They aren't going to cut you a check overnight. It'll take time, lots and lots of time. You'll have to prove that these men are dead. You'll have to argue in court that your father's stipulation has been fulfilled. And then you'll have to prove that you are indeed the sole and rightful heir, and so on and so forth. It could take years. This person who has done all your dirty work for you so that you can get your inheritance, is he supposed to wait around trusting that someday, if and when you finally get your loot, that you'll live up to whatever deal is worked out? Ma'am, you must take me for a fool."

"No, sir. I don't. If such a person agreed to such a contract a firm dollar amount would be offered, a dollar amount that is readily available, some of which could be given in advance. The contractor would not have to worry about the inheritance, having already been paid."

"And what dollar amount would that be?"

"Ten thousand a head."

"And you have fifty thousand dollars?"

"I most certainly do."

"In that case your inheritance must be much, much more than that!"

"And that would be my business, but even if I never receive a nickel of that inheritance, the contractor will still have been paid, and it would have been worth it to me to get these scumbags who killed Patty off the street."

"I remind you ma'am," I said, using a folded up

napkin found in my trench coat to wipe some leakage away from the side of my PV, "that we are merely talking in hypotheticals. I have not agreed to any such contract. I'm going to have to ask you to leave now. I have my own problems."

She stood. "I assure you, my money is green and orange." She reached under her dress, into her bra, and pulled out some crisp green and orange bills, five hundred dollars, flinging it down onto the open manila folder. "That puts you under no obligation. It's merely for your time. I'll leave the folder. After you've studied it, if you decide all you want is that" (referring to the $500) "then shred or burn the contents of the folder. My contact information is there. I'm staying in a motel on Lincoln Avenue. Now please, if you don't mind, I'll need a little help climbing down out of here." I held what felt like leather under her white gloves as she stepped down through the trap and gained her footing on the ladder. She climbed down and called out, "Thank you for your time, Mr. Provario."

Now that I recall it, it briefly dawned upon me that Vera made it through her spiel without stuttering once, but my suspicion was forgotten with the feeling of five crisp one hundred dollar bills in my hand. Ah, but you know me my dear, that money didn't last long. Soon I was back at the public library, using their free internet service, browsing around the Vape Mania forum, looking for advice on do-it-yourself e-juice, since I had come across a bottle of orange extract from a little shop in Chinatown and had also discovered a tube of vegetable glycerin next to a pair of handcuffs in a drawer of the nightstand in Brandon's Dads' bedroom.

"When are you going to get rid of that old hat?" someone whispered to me.

I had been on the lookout for that Vaporazzi jerk

Mike Crow, who had identified me while I was sitting in that very spot, while also hiding from the librarian, who had threatened to have me arrested; so, startled and defensive I turned and snarled. But it was Elle, sitting there smiling like a munchkin, with her hair now dyed green, wearing a Cotton Spandex Sleeveless Crop Top from American Apparel (I recognized it from the catalogue I enjoyed reading while sitting on the Bieberman toilet). She had no bra on underneath, which I thought was liberating, and she wore tan Khaki Shorts.

"I like this hat," I said.

"Unfortunately so do the moths."

"So, moths have to eat too."

I made her laugh and this pleased me. I'm confident that you are a mature, rational person, my dear Yugo, without a jealous bone in your body; so, yes, I admit I had a crush on Elle. We began playfully insulting each other's clothe (I called her Laura Croft and she called me Indiana Jones) but it became obvious our chatter was disturbing the library, so we slipped on out. She told me that she only had a few minutes since she was interning for a distinguished Professor named Chas Fraloupka at UIC's Institute for Health Research and Policy, who was working on a study concerning the economics of tobacco and tobacco control. The professor was presently in Tanzania, so Elle was very busy in his office answering his phone taking messages and would need to get back. Discovering that we were less than a mile from each other, we promised to hook up again, and in an excited way I purchased some time for my cell phone and tidied up my crawlspace in anticipation, and I wasn't let down, since she called me the next day. I quickly gave her the Bieberman phone number so that I didn't use up my minutes, and I hurried down the hatch and into the house as the phone was ringing. I called out, "That's for me!" and took the phone into the pantry, where I closed myself in, sat on the floor and had a long, flirtatious conversation during which my heart started opening up so widely I was afraid the fruit flies might swarm in.

Brandon eventually tapped his knuckles on the pantry door and informed me that he was expecting a call from his Dads, so I asked if Elle wanted to stop by and help me make some do-it-yourself e-juice. I opened the pantry door and handed the phone to BB, who was wearing a red, white and blue speedo that was so tight the contours of his veins were visible. "Bro you're glowing like a tanning bed. Who's the biatch?" Brandon made me blush. "Well look at you," he said, whacking the side of my arm with his palm so hard that some dust puffed off my trench coat. "I knew you had it in you."

I was glad for that pat on my arm. It meant things were okay. The day before, when I got back from the library, I was in his kitchen trying out my veggy glycerin and orange extract concoction. Using hypodermic blunt needles, I put 10% orange oil into a 15 milliliter plastic bottle, and then I put in 65% VG and then 25% of a 100mg nicotine solution that I had stored in the Bieberman freezer. I shook the mixture up and then plopped it into the microwave to give it a quick ten second steeping, but I must have pressed the wrong buttons, because when I went to the sink to wash out my measuring gear as the microwave hummed, there was an alarming pop like a burst balloon. I flinched and swung around to discover the inside of the microwave on fire. Flames were licking out of the side vents as I rushed to get the fire extinguisher. Finding it, I pulled the pin, popped the oven door open with a swift kick from the tip of my shoe, sending a ball of black smoke and flame blowing out, and I gave it and long blast, extinguishing the fire. The microwave was ruined, its black and flaking ceiling hanging in solidified plastic bubbles, and soot stained the wall and cabinets above it. I left Brandon a note apologizing for the incident and promised to replace the oven, but he was nevertheless pissed. I could hear him cursing and slamming things around below me as I hid in the attic. I tell you, Yugo, I expected to get evicted. But he calmed down and finally shouted up at me, "Dude you gots ta be more careful. My Dads are gonna kill me for this!" Now he stood there in his speedo congratulating me on finding love, the charred microwave in the alley sticking out of a big plastic garbage can.

This made Brandon especially cool in my book considering the microwave incident happened on top of the hole I made in the ceiling. I haven't mentioned that yet, have I? I woke up in the middle of the night on my futon mattress, half asleep and irritable due to the bed bugs, and I thought I heard the hoot of an owl. Walking toward the sound and shining my little Empire Mods keychain light around, I discovered it to be a big white rat in heat, moaning through two long teeth from the top of a supporting beam. I stepped away onto an area of the floor where there was a gap between two pieces of plywood and I fell through the ceiling and landed on Brandon's Dads' bed below. Brandon came rushing through the house in the nude, crying, "What the hell was that?" He flicked on the light and saw me, covered in dust and insulation with pieces of drywall splattered on his Dads' bed and he looked up and saw the gaping hole in the ceiling. "My Dads are gonna kill me!" he cried out. I assured him that by the time his Dads got back from India, I would have my settlement check and would hire someone to make the ceiling as good as new.

Elle began making regular visits to my crawlspace. I knew she was there when I heard her secret knock on the trap, playing I Wanna Be Sedated with her knuckles against the plywood. At first I was afraid that when she saw the way I lived she'd freak out and cut all ties with me; but on the contrary, she found it groovy, and started decorating my place with Misfits posters and she even strung a set of skull lights across the length of the attic.

"So what are these things?" she asked as she snooped around while I lie on my futon mattress and vaped. She was hunched over the work table that I had constructed out of two by fours, on which the gadgets I had invented were.

"That's the Melvin Line, my own brand of personal vaping devices," I said. "Someday I'll patent them and I'll get rich, but they still need tweaking."

"What's this one do?" she asked, picking up what must have appeared to her to be just a tin can with a drip tip sticking out of it.

"That's the MP-900 Lung Saver, a self-vaping cartomizer," I said. "It's got a little fan in it that sucks the vapor for you and shoots it out the drip tip for the perfect vape every time. Wait—" I said as she flicked the switch. Thick licorice flavored vapor came pouring out of it. "Oh Nilly now you've done it."

"Juniper. That's pretty cool," she said, flicking the switch to the off position, but the vapor didn't stop coming out; instead, it grew thicker and spewed out more rapidly.

"That's what I was about to say. Something's wrong with it," and I crawled over to take it from her. I rapidly flicked the switch back and forth as blinding vapor filled the attic. Elle waved her hands in front of her face, trying to see. "You kind of have to, here, like this, you just have to do it," and as I attempted to jimmy the switch, the MP-900 fumbled out of my hands. I attempted to save it with my foot as if it was a bean bag but that just sent it tumbling into the hole.

"Brandon's gonna kill me," I said and I put my arms to my sides like a plank and hopped in after it, falling through the fog onto the bed below with a bounce that sent me crashing against the headboard. I retrieved the gadget and unscrewed the cap and the four batteries inside of it tumbled out, stopping the vapor from spewing.

Elle poked her face into the hole in the ceiling. "So you invented a smoke bomb," she said.

"Vape bomb," I corrected. "Like I said, it needs tweaking."

Unfortunately for him, Roger Zigfield didn't know how to stop the licorice flavored vapor when Mr. Vape tossed the MP-900 Lung Saver into his car. Mr. Vape was stalking him from a distance at the Hills of Peace Cemetery in Joliet. Phil and Larry and Red had just finished burying their brother Danny. They stood around in their poorly fitted suits arguing with each as he watched them through a pair of binoculars. They eventually split up and got in their cars and went their separate ways. Mr. Vape tailed Red in the Toyota Camry that he borrowed from Uncle Nick's secret lot, using a license plate from a Kia that was parked at the Walmart Neighborhood Center. Red was in his metallic blue Chrysler 200. Just as Vera predicted he would, Red got off Route 66 to take a shortcut through an isolated stretch of Cass Road that was surrounded by forest preserve. Mr. Vape held Vera's radio transmitter on his lap as the two cars ventured deeper into the woods on a peaceful road that was covered with red and yellow leaves, the sun flickering between the trees.

Mr. Vape flipped the toggle switch that activated the mechanism that severed the break line in Red's car. Then Mr. Vape sped up and pulled beside Red and honked his horn to gain his attention and motioned with his hand for him to roll his window down; and when Red reluctantly did with a press of a button and the brown blotch marks on his face were confirmed, Mr. Vape shouted, "Have a vape!" and tossed the vape bomb in. The inside of the car immediately began filling with vapor, blinding Red. Within the vapor there was a flash of yellow light and then it seemed to Mr. Vape that everything began moving in slowed motion, the microseconds flipping like film frames, until the bullet skimmed the windshield of the Camry leaving a streak of shattered glass, releasing time back to its normal speed. Mr. Vape slowed and maneuvered behind Red and flipped the switch that would cause the Chrysler's accelerator to jam. The Chrysler jerked forward and continued to speed up as Red attempted to roll down all his windows to clear the air, vapor pouring out of the sides of his car. There was another yellow flash inside the car and the rear window shattered and a hole popped into Mr. Vape's windshield as the bullet whistled past his head. Mr. Vape swerved the Camry from side to side to avoid the bullets, nearly losing control, as Red blindly unloaded his gun at him.

But it was already too late for Red. Cass turned sharply to the right at the entrance to the biking trail, where the sycamore had stood for the last century. Mr. Vape slammed on his breaks, skidding to a halt, as Red screamed out horrifically before slamming the Chrysler into the tree with a boom that could be heard for miles. Mr. Vape slowly drove by the smoking, mangled vehicle that was wrapped onto the tree like a big blue burl. Behind the shattered windshield, it looked like someone had tossed a plate of spaghetti. Mr. Vape had to be completely sure, so he pulled over, hopped out and ran over to the wreckage to have a quick peek, confirming the air bags malfunctioned as Vera promised they would. There was no way the broken and mangled pile of flesh inside was still alive.

I heard a creaking. "Shhhhhh," I blew. We waited—me on Brandon's Dads' bed and Elle with her head poking through the ceiling, until the vapor dissipated. I rounded up my Lung Saver and batteries and shoved them in my trench coat pockets and rolled off the bed. On the floor I discovered a framed photo of the Dads. They weren't what I had imagined them to be. Dad #1 was elderly with obvious false teeth with the middle of his skull bald, and Dad #2 looked about twenty years younger and was Asian. Asian Dad rested the side of his head on elderly Dad's shoulder. Both smiled widely. Behind them there was a body of water with a sailboat on it, and in front of them there was a crack in the glass over the photo. I would need to get it fixed before Brandon found out, so I shoved the photo in my thigh pocket, snuck out of the room, crept through the hall, skipped downstairs, out the back door, up the back porch and up the aluminum ladder back into the attic.

"That was freaky," Elle said. She was back at my work table perusing my gadgets. She picked up a harmonica and asked, "So what does this do, vape while you play it?"

"No, that's just a harmonica, but, hmmm, you may have something there."

"How about this," she said, pointing to a long contraption. It housed a lawnmower battery connected to an engine salvaged from a leaf blower, over a 500 milliliter plastic bottle filled with bubblegum flavored e-juice. A rubber hose came out of the bottle and fit snugly into a length of copper piping.

"That! That, my dear Elle, is the MP-FUK-ALL. When I get it fine-tuned the FUK-ALL will be the guts of *thee* world's largest e-hookah. The little engine there pumps the e-juice out of the bottle and sends it up through this copper pipe, inside of which is a series of microcoils and wicks. It will produce enough vapor to fill a giant hookah with a dozen hoses on it, so everyone can sit around and vape from it."

"Does it work?" she asked.

"I just did some tweaking on it this morning, so let's give it a whirl," I said. I lifted the heavy, bulky gadget, wrapping my left arm around the housing with the battery and motor, snuggling the bottle of juice against my hip, with the rubber hose draped across my neck and the copper pipe held in my right hand like an insecticide dispenser. I flicked the switch with my thumb and the motor began whirring and the juice in the bottle started bubbling and the rubber hose started jerking and there came a horrible sizzling noise from inside the copper and Elle, just in the nick of time, grabbed it and pointed it at the little open window as a stream of flaming e-juice squirted out of it. The fountain of flame went out the window, expanding into a rain of fire drops as the juice fell in a long, splattering parabola all over the apple tree in the backyard. The tree was set ablaze as the e-juice clung to it like napalm. "Oh crap!" we jinxed each other.

Brandon came running out of the house, holding a big container of Gatorade. "You've got to be kidding me!" he called out as he attempted in vain to douse the flames with his sports drink.

"BB, I'm so sorry," I cried out the window.

He stood there looking up at me, his palms lifted above his head as if he was doing some type of Hindu dance, the tree burning and crackling behind him. Then he came marching up the back porch stairs and shouted at me to come down. I thumped the cover off the hatch and came sliding down the ladder.

"My Dads are going to kill me!" he shouted into my face like a drill sergeant.

"I don't know what to say," I said as glowing embers fell off the tree.

"A flame thrower dog? Really?" he squealed.

"No, it's not a flame thrower. It's an e-hookah. It malfunctioned. Listen, pal, I was trying to impress Elle."

"And wazzup wit dat?" he said, his eyes bugging as if he was going to explode. "How old is that girl anyway? She looks like she belongs in grade school."

"Oh, she's eighteen," I assured him.

"Sure?"

"Don't worry, I carded her," I said.

"You carded her??" he squealed in astonishment, and he paced back and forth in a state of confusion before he approached again and spoke in a hush so Elle didn't hear. "Even true that, it's creepy like Jackson man. I mean, come on dog, what are you, like in you forties?"

"Come on pal," I said, grabbing his bicep and giving him a little massage. "Don't be like that. We haven't been doing anything, you know what I mean, and even if we do there's no law against it. We're just friends, don't sweat it. Listen, BB, trust me, I'm going to make everything okay. When I get my settlement check, well don't you worry, pal. We're going to get you a new microwave, and that hole in the ceiling is getting fixed, and—" I looked at the tree that was now bald and smoking. "Listen, I'm supposed to get that settlement check any day now."

"Man you gots ta be more careful. You know you my bro but you gots ta be more careful," he said, jerking to one side as if his leg had turned into a spring.

"Let's have a hug," I said and we embraced. I squeezed him tight and made sure he heard how good it made me feel. He squeezed back tighter, angrily, stopping me from breathing for a moment, before he violently let go, nudging me away with his chest. "We'll cut it down," I panted. "When your Dads get home, tell 'em it got struck by lightning." I offered him a fist bump.

"Man, you got answers for everything. I can't believe this shit," and Brandon smacked my fist so hard my knuckles would swell. "And what you mean *we'll* cut it down. I can't believe this shit," he repeated in frustration and marched away down the stairs.

My Dear Yugo, please don't think badly of me, but I was merely buying time. I had no idea when that settlement check was coming, and even if Brandon was an odd bird and one heck of a pushover, I had grown fond of him and felt sorry for him. He was going to be in a lot of trouble when his Dads got home. My monthly disability check was nearly used up and I had spent Vera Grimmel's money on some bad ass tanks and mods that I wish I had time to describe for you, and I wasn't getting any calls from my local shopper ad. I feared if I didn't find some money soon, not only would I betray my friend BB but Elle might lose interest in me as well, so I guess that's why that folder with the information about the five Zigfield brothers started nagging at me.

I started taking it out just to amuse myself, and

found myself really disliking their faces. Each one of them possessed some trait, some look in his eye or smirk or wrinkling of the brow that truly appalled me. Phil was the worst of them, a really mean looking son of a bridge with a face that looked like tree bark with a scar running across it. There I was, with all the information about their secret operation. Perhaps I was only one of a handful of people on earth who knew these details. But how much of it was even true? Could I trust this woman whose makeup looked like it was applied by Homer Simpson? Bootleg cigarettes? I had never heard of such a thing. Was distributing bootleg cigarettes even worth the risks? Could such a scheme even be profitable?

I stood in a Snake Eyes convenience store, browsing some magazines and reading the fine print on every last package of beef jerky. What I was really doing was observing the cashier. Something fishy was going on. Not all purchases of cigarettes were rung up at the cash register; some of them were being rung up on an adding machine that spit out a strip of paper that was torn off and handed over as a receipt only when it was requested. In twenty minutes alone there were sixteen purchases of cigarettes, seven of which were suspect. I got a jumbo slushy freeze and did the math. If in this one Snake Eyes store alone, seven bootleg packs of cigarettes were sold in twenty minutes, that would be twenty-one in the hour, perhaps 300 packs a day taking into account slow evening hours. That's 2100 packs of counterfeit cigarettes a week, or roughly 110,000 packs a year, at about $10 a pack—that's $1,100,000 per year. And that was only *one store*. There must be fifty, maybe sixty Snake Eyes stores in Chicago. Surely, these petty crooks who couldn't even manage to keep their private information out of the hands of Vera

Grimmel weren't operating a fifty million dollar a year business. No. They would have to give the franchise owners a cut, probably half the profits, and surely they didn't have every Snake Eyes store under their thumb, probably just a dozen or so. But still. Even chipping it away like that, it still could be millions that the brothers divvied up every year.

Mr. Vape began talking in my head. What if I was capable of pulling it off? How would I do it? Mr. Vape orchestrated many fantastic, cinematic scenes in my mind in which I assassinated five hard core criminals; but they were all too wild and weren't satisfying and I realized why. I had never met any of them. They were cartoon characters in my fantasies, nothing but smudgy color copies on pieces of paper. How could I possibly satisfy my imagination without coming into physical contact with them? It was folly, of course. I was no killer; perhaps I have a bad temper that at times sends me into psychotic rages, but premeditated murder? The seed had been planted, however. Thinking about it gave me some purpose, was something to do, at least, as I hid in the attic and vaped.

I decided I would choose one of the brothers and set out to meet him. No, not just meet him, make physical contact with him — shake a hand or brush arms with him. It was a challenge. I looked through Vera's file, and after reading their information for the twentieth time, I decided Larry Zigfield would be the easiest to meet. Roger ran a tobacco shop and I no longer smoked, I vaped, so what would be the premise of my visit? Danny was out in the southwest suburbs and Bart was secure in a hospice and I wasn't ready to stroll on into Smokey's Tavern. So I set out on a quest to touch Larry Zigfield.

He wasn't difficult to find. Ziggy Light's was listed

in the phonebook, on Lawrence near Kimball. I looked up Larry's hours of business and contemplated the best time to go. Weekends might be too busy. I didn't want a lot of people in the store; it would be better to have some alone time, to observe, perhaps engage him in conversation, to get close enough to touch him. Evenings might get busy for him as well, when everyone gets off work. I admit, my dear Yugo, it was exciting, working it out in my mind. Maybe during the morning would be best. Not right after he opens when he might be preoccupied with something, but perhaps an hour later, after he's settled in, when business is still slow. What day of the week? Tuesday sounded good. Why not *this* Tuesday.

So on Tuesday morning when Brandon was at boy band rehearsal, I borrowed his Diamondback road bike and walked it out of the gangway to the street, where I noticed some people looking at the house. I turned to see that someone had spray painted

A RAPIST LIVES HERE

on the white steel siding under the bow window. Was Brandon a rapist? I had seen no evidence of this but regardless, I was sure Brandon's Dads were going to kill him for it anyway.

I decided to take the Lake Michigan bike path since I seldom get to the lake. I'm not that fond of open spaces and I have to be in quite a specific mood to enjoy them, but when I am in that mood, oh Yugo, it is refreshing and inspirational and reminds me of you. I really should have been spending all my spare time down there whenever I managed to get out of bed. It was a long trek up north and I stopped to observe the beauty on several occasions, mainly to kill time since it was still early. I exited on Lawrence and rode to the west. As you recall, we had a weird summer last year and it was warmer in October than it was in May, and the city air was getting hotter and more humid the farther away I got from the lake. I rode through Uptown (that's a crazy place!) through Lincoln Square (the middle class Lincoln Park) and up into an unfamiliar neighborhood that was ethnically mixed with Greeks and middle easterners.

There it was, Ziggy Light's. It looked typical for a liquor store, with lots of posters in the windows for different brands of alcohol, advertising sale prices with a few neon signs as well. I leaned Brandon's Diamondback against a pay to park box and I'll be honest, I felt giddy as I walked inside. I was impressed. I was expecting something sleazy, but Larry Zigfield had a really nice establishment, with a huge selection of microbrews and an entire aisle of wine, with another aisle for groceries. Next to the checkout counter there was a glass display case with various lunchmeats and cheeses and a sign on the wall pricing sandwiches. Some guy with pitch black hair who had dandruff was sitting on a stool behind the checkout. I knew it wasn't Larry but just to reassure myself, I got Vera's sheet out of my back pocket and unfolded it to look at the photo.

I got a ginger beer and paid for it, and then I asked, "Can I get a pastrami on rye?" I was being rather cunning since I had observed the tray marked pastrami was empty. My impromptu plan worked like a charm. The man asked me to wait a moment as he rung up another customer and then he went to the deli counter and, seeing that there was no pastrami, he briefly went through an opening of hanging pvc strips then he came out and politely asked if I could wait a moment; and then, sure enough, out came Larry, sideburns and all, a lot smaller than I thought he would be. He wore a white apron and carried a tray of freshly sliced pastrami that reflected off his huge pair of eyeglasses. He set the tray into the deli display and as he did so, I saw the Ziggy tattoo on his left hand, on the skin between his thumb and pointer, just before he snapped on a pair of thin rubber gloves. It was just as Vera had described: a Z with a cigarette through it like an inverted dollar sign. It also had a scribble coming off the top of it representing a waft of smoke.

"Been here long?" I asked.

"Since ninety-nine. Dark or light?"

I shrugged. He gestured to the bread. "Dark sounds good. This place reminds me of a place where I use to get schnitzels."

"Nope, no schnitzel," he said, working on my sandwich like a real pro. "Mustard?"

"Yes, of course," I said.

"Hot or mild?"

"Yes, mild, mild."

In one smooth, continuous motion he reached back and pulled a strip of thick white paper off a roll, yanked it with a zip against a jagged metal strip, put the piece of paper on the counter in front of him and put my sandwich on it and then held it lovingly with one hand as if cupping a breast as he sliced the sandwich in two; he plopped a quarter of a pickle next to it, wrapped it up in the paper, pulled a piece of masking tape off a spool and sealed the package, retrieving a pencil from behind his ear in a flash and jotting something onto the paper; and then he asked, "Anything else?"

"Hmmm," I hummed, stalling over the deli. He was going to hand my sandwich to the cashier. I wanted him to hand it directly to me. So I slowly reached my arm out as I stared at the glass as if contemplating, and he resisted for a second before surrendering. He reached over the deli counter to hand me the sandwich and as I took it from him my thumb touched his thumb and Mr. Vape shouted at me, "No, not good enough! Flesh on rubber doesn't count," so I fumbled with the sandwich, nearly dropping it, and he saved it with both hands and offered it to me firmly as my fingers brushed the hair on the back of his wrist. "No, I think that'll be it. Thanks!"

"You're welcome," he said. "N-joy!"

I paid for my sandwich and went outside to sit at the bus stop and eat. I drank my ginger beer, smiling to myself. That? That was the scary mean evil dangerous Larry Zigfield who deserved to die? He looked like he weighed ninety pounds and was so polite, a bit curt and to the point, but polite nonetheless; and the sandwich, oh the sandwich, he made it with such loving care, packed with pastrami on the freshest bread with a nice crisp pickle, and all for only $4.95. How could someone who makes a sandwich like that be evil? Even if it was true, that somewhere in that back room of his there was something dubious going on, so what? What business was that of mine? Should that be a death sentence?

I was amused but something nagged at me. I knew that what I had just done, purposely meeting this man face to face and intentionally getting close enough to touch him, wouldn't have been done if Mr. Vape wasn't entertaining Vera Grimmel's proposal. I sat there nodding then shaking my head, as I argued with him. Sure, fifty thousand dollars would solve a lot of problems, but even that, *only* fifty thousand dollars for murdering five people? Mr. Vape agreed it should be more. I insisted that I wasn't actually considering doing it, not even considering *considering* doing it. What I just did was merely a game. It was a test of my wits and nerve. Mr. Vape argued back. Why didn't I get butterflies in my stomach, then, and lose my cool, like I did when I confronted those harmless dweebs at the vape den, he wanted to know. And he was right. A moment ago, when confronting what I was told was a notorious villain, I was in complete control. There wasn't a stutter coming out of my mouth, nor any hesitation or concern. I finished my sandwich and, not seeing a waste basket, I rolled up the paper and shoved it in the pocket of my trench coat.

I sat there having a vape. Mr. Vape was scaring me. What if he was right? What if this wasn't just some silly game? What if Mr. Vape really was contemplating murder? Even if he was, surely I, the me who is me, wasn't, not after meeting the man and seeing how harmless he appeared to be. But was he harmless? I was his customer so of course he was being polite to me. Maybe he just likes making sandwiches. Maybe that's what keeps the evil voices in his head from ranting and raving. I vape and he makes sandwiches. He had the tattoo just like Vera said he would have. I couldn't exactly walk in there and demand to see his back room. If I wanted to do that, I'd have to create a diversion, or break in after hours. See! Right there! Why was I thinking like that if Mr. Vape wasn't considering it?

My problems splashed like a stormy sea in my mind. What was I going to do about that tree that I burned down? What was going to happen when the Bieberman Dads got home? I'd be out on the street again. Where would I go? The money would help. But no! It was ridiculous. I told Mr. Vape to get it out of my mind. You wouldn't be able to pull it off even once, let alone *five times*, I scolded him; and for a lousy fifty thousand? I bet I could get a hundred thousand off Vera, easily. We agreed on one thing at least. It would be one hundred thousand dollars or nothing.

I laughed audibly and mumbled to myself. Sure, I could see myself killing someone. People kill people all the time. If I was being mugged, for example, I think I could pull the Innokin VTR out of my pocket and bash someone's face in with it; or, if someone was threatening Granmama. Oh poor Granmama. How long would she last before she needed to go into a home? And who would pay for that? A hundred thousand dollars could pay for that. I shook my head angrily and growled. I'm not doing this, I scolded. I'm not wasting my mental energy on *you*. I tried to force myself to think about productive things. Think about vaping, I told myself, think about vaping. But the only thing that came to mind was an article I recently read claiming there is formaldehyde in it. Maybe I was smoking embalming fluid. Could embalming fluid bring out the evil intentions and turn them into the faces in the sidewalk that I wanted to smash? Ah flood it. I had another vape.

I was sure the Zigfields *did* have something shady going on. Maybe they *were* into bootlegging. But who was I to judge? I had no proof that they killed Vera's brother. Why should I be the angel of vape? I laughed out loud again. I meant to think angel of death, but I was taking a nice vape at the moment so the words in my mind got mixed up.

I slapped myself on the head nearly knocking off my trilby. A thought came to me. If this guy was so normal looking, then maybe the rest of the Ziggies were normal. Maybe Vera intentionally gave me bad photos of them snarling in order to manipulate me. Maybe if I met the rest of them, I'd see the truth, that Vera has some grudge that has nothing to do with me. Maybe that would convince Mr. Vape that what he was considering was lunacy. Hell, why even bother meeting all of them? I just needed to meet the one that Vera described as the devil himself. He was supposed to be the worst of the worst, so if Phil Zigfield turned out to be just some average joe politely serving drinks at his tavern, then that would be proof enough.

That's what I would do then, I decided. I'd go to Smokey's Tavern. I'd see if I could pull off the same stunt with Smokey. Meet him. Have a conversation with him. Get close enough to touch him. How risky could it be? Mr. Vape had to be dealt with, had to be put in his place, had to be silenced once and for all before he persistently nudged and nagged at me like a little bitch until I did his will.

I was sitting there for quite some time, so a few busses had passed as I was waving my arms around mumbling to myself, blowing vapor out of my mouth, but the next bus that pulled up opened its doors. I waved my hand at the bus driver instructing him to drive on but he just looked forward as the back door flipped open and out came Mike Crow, who stood there as the bus hissed and drove away. I clenched my fists. Mike held up his palms in peace. "Now don't get hot headed," he said. "I saw you sitting there and I just want to talk."

"I have nothing to say to you. And if you know what's good for you, you won't pull out that camera."

"Well about that camera, you know you, that camera was, oh, what's the point? Never mind. Listen Melvin, another bus should be coming in about twenty minutes and I promise I'll get on it and leave you alone. That's all I'm asking for. Twenty minutes of your time." I looked away and shook my head. "Can I sit?" he asked.

"It's a public bench," I said.

Mike sat down, leaving as much space on the

bench between us as he could. He smelled like patchouli, making me wonder what a patchouli vape would taste like. "I know you don't think much of what I do, but I help bring vaping into the mainstream. Nobody cares about a scene where people just wash each other's backs. Nobody cares about a private club. I treat vaping as news worthy, so news worthy that it deserves its own gossip column. And that makes people perk up and take notice. Honestly, I started out writing positive reviews but nobody read them. The first time I wrote a piece that was a bit scandalous, that poked fun at the vaping culture, that treated vapers like celebrities who can survive a bit of ridicule, I suddenly got thousands of hits."

"Well good for you!" I spat at him. "You and the jerks who killed Diana."

"I don't harbor any ill intentions toward you," he said. "I'm actually here to help. You should take advantage of me, you know, to tell your side of the story."

"And what story is that?"

"I've only heard stuff secondhand, and that's why it would be interesting to hear your side of the story, but the story goes you encouraged Francesco Constantine to launch that study into vaping, and now that's being used as the main argument to regulate it, and in some cases, even to ban it."

"That's a lie! I never encouraged anything. I gave him some juice to test because it tasted like ass and I wanted to know what was in it. He needed something to do for his senior thesis and had waited until the last minute. He's the one who decided to take it one step further."

He cleared his throat. "Fair enough. We're just two men talking. But, you know, you do look a little down and out. My website, you know, it isn't doing half bad. Sometimes I'm actually able to pay people for interviews."

"This isn't an interview and you better not quote me. I'll deny everything. What do you mean you pay people? How much?"

There was a sudden chill in the air and I noticed an ominous gray cloud forming to the west.

"For an interview with the notorious Melvin Provario? I'd pay two hundred dollars."

"And what happens after I spend that two hundred dollars and my face is still plastered all over your website. Do people throw their cartos at me on the street?"

"We could do a video interview. Real professional like. That way you'd be assured you wouldn't be misquoted."

"Would you blur my face and disguise my voice?"

"That actually might be pretty cool."

"So you'd really pay me three hundred dollars to be videotaped with my identity disguised?"

"Are we negotiating now?"

"Is there a *we* now?"

"But why blur your face? When you testify before the joint commission they aren't going to blur your face, and that'll be aired nationally on C-SPAN. We'd definitely have to do it before that."

"I'm not testifying at that witch hunt," I assured him.

"You're listed as one of the witnesses. I'm sure you've been subpoenaed."

"Let them try to find me."

"I found you."

"Listen, Mac or Mike or whatever the vape your name is," I said angrily. "I said I'm not testifying at any vaping hearing. Ha. The CTA is early for once. Here comes your bus." I waved at the bus and it pulled up and it hissed as its doors opened. "I'll think about it, Mac. I know how to get ahold of you. It's double-u double-u double-u jerkoff. Now get on the bus!" Mike Crow stepped up onto the bus reluctantly and as the doors closed in front of him he called out, "E-mail me!"

When the bus was out of sight, I mounted Brandon's Diamondback and started biking farther north. At one point in my journey the bottom of my trench coat got stuck in the chain and I had to stop and untangle it. The dark cloud that was approaching from the west now enveloped half the sky and a chilly breeze was threatening to blow my trilby off.

Ziggy Light's may have impressed me, but Smokey's Tavern was just what I imagined it to be: a real shit hole. It was a big square cinderblock box with one darkly tinted window in it. By the time I got there, a sprinkling was blowing horizontally and leaves were falling off the trees. Then the sky split open with a flash and an ear splitting crack popped against my face and all hell broke loose. The rain came in huge droplets that lost their individuality as water gushed down drenching me. I came up to the door of the tavern thinking they might let me bring the bike inside but the door was locked. It was a thick, solid door with a little diamond shaped window in it that I peered through. I could only make out a bit of the room but it was clear there were people inside, and I could hear electronic dance music thumping as well. I tried knocking but I hurt my knuckles. Nobody heard me and I knew if I pounded too desperately I would inspire nothing but suspicion, so I decided to seek shelter.

I went around the block to the alley in back of Smokey's and found a door sunk in the wall, allowing just enough space in its frame to take refuge after hiding Brandon's bike under some cardboard behind a garbage dumpster. After I had a few vapes, the storm subsided, leaving the sky dark gray and sprinkling. I was on the verge of deciding that today was not the best day to visit Smokey. All I felt like doing was making my way home and having a nap in the attic. As the rain slowed into a light shower, I came out of my vaping hole and right then, behind me, I could hear something banging lightly against the door; then I heard keys jingling.

I stepped away from the building and nonchalantly walked, my head bowed, my eyes peeking out from under the brim of my hat, as the steel door opened. Someone came out lugging a big black plastic bag. He flung the top of the dumpster open, whacking the brick wall behind it, as he flipped the bag over his shoulder and tossed it in with the sound of bottles clanking, and he rushed back inside, leaving the door open. It was providence, clearly a sign. What were the chances the door would open at the very moment when I was about to give up? I cautiously approached and peered in. It was a storage room, filled with cases of beer. I stepped inside and heard footsteps approaching, so I dashed behind a tower of boxes and hid. The man proceeded with another bag and tossed it into the dumpster and he lit a cigarette before he stepped inside, slamming the door shut. When he was gone, I realized I had not thought any of this through, and I completely chickened out, attempting an escape, but the door was locked and I wasn't the one with the key.

I crept toward the swinging door that the man had gone through, pushing it slightly open to peek, the electronic music growing louder as I did. There was a bar with three people sitting at it, behind which was a man made out of boulders who was drying out the inside of a beer pitcher with a towel. To the right there were two well-dressed men sitting at a booth against the sole window, looking as if they were discussing something very grim. Further to the right, there was a little dance floor with a disco ball hanging above it, with a wall of mirrored tiles and colored lights pointing down from the ceiling. Nobody was on it. It was still early. The music screeched like a power drill over and over as a beat thumped and a frantic synthesized horn played like some wired up bumblebee. I could see a glare coming through the diamond shaped window; the sun was coming out.

I went back into the storage room and contemplated over a vape. I couldn't exactly walk out there with so few people in the room. I would be noticed straight away. I'd have to wait until things started picking up. Then I could slip into the bar unnoticed and mingle through the crowd before escaping out the front door. But what time would that be? And did the joint even pick up at all on a Tuesday? And what about Brandon's bicycle? I was in a dilemma, but all I could do was crawl into a corner behind the boxes and vape it out.

As the afternoon dragged on, people sporadically arrived. Once in a while I crept out to take a peek. I discovered that the people were being let in by means of a buzzer that the bartender activated for them, only after he verified who was outside by means of a video monitor that he had with him behind the bar. So there was a camera outside. So maybe he did hear me knocking. Maybe he purposely didn't let me in. So what was going to happen if I walked out there and he recognized me as the guy he *didn't* let in? Another thing struck me as I was peeking. Everyone was smoking cigarettes. There were even ashtrays on the bar and tables. Apparently the clean indoor ordinance didn't apply to Smokey's. That place was clearly above the law.

With the passing of every hour the music was turned up a notch, and the light near the dance floor was dimmed, and once in a while a strobe light would flash for a minute or two. At about six o'clock the place was getting packed with people and there was a topless woman wearing a G-string serving drinks and another one pole dancing in a little elevated corner. It was as if the scariest looking people in Chicago were being bussed to Smokey's Tavern. Some of them looked like they belonged in Las Angeles, with shaved heads and tattoos all over their bodies, but others looked like they belonged in a Martin Scorsese film, wearing suits, their collars tightly buttoned under their chiseled faces. One of them seemed to look at me as I peeped, causing me to rush around looking for a place to urinate. All the women in the joint were hookers, plain and simple. None of the men were with any of them. They shouted at them and laughed and slapped them on their asses and grabbed them and groped them and then there were three topless waitresses and by nine o'clock some woman was on her knees with her head bobbing between the legs of some disgusting fat guy at the crowded bar.

At midnight I made my move. I slipped out of the storage room and shimmied through the crowd, jerking my shoulders up and down and to and fro to the music that was now blasting. The dance floor was invaded by intoxicated people who were moving around listlessly as if struggling to digest their Quaaludes. I twirled on my toes, flipping my trench coat around like a cape, bending my knees and jerking my hips to the delight of everyone, male and female, who danced with me, as I moved toward the front door. A group of people were huddled around a man with a huge beige cheroot held between his legs, with a line of coke on it from its end to his crotch. "Do it. Do it. Do it," they cheered as some skank with hula-hoops hanging from her ears got down on her knees and stuck a straw in her nose and sucked the coke away. Everyone cheered and I gave them my thumbs up and cheered along with them. I could see on the monitor behind the bar that the bouncers outside the club were tossing some dweeb back and forth amongst themselves as if passing a ball. They finally pushed him, tripping him with their feet. He stumbled, fell on his face and then crawled away as the buzzer went off and the door opened and some more people poured in. That was my opportunity. As the door was open, I acted like I recognized someone and waved my hand and rushed toward the door to escape, when someone grabbed me around my shoulder and said into my ear, "There you are. Diplazzio's waiting for you."

A tall man with ears like corn tortillas brought me to the booth next to the window where three men were sitting. With a nudge to my shoulder, he instructed me to sit down with them. There was one beside me and two facing me. I looked at them from under my trilby tipped over my brow. The guy directly in front of me had an eyeball that was white and lifeless. He looked at me with his other eye in anticipation. The guy sitting next to him kept pushing the broken neon Blatz sign in the window aside so he could look out. The guy who brought me to the table hovered over me like an awning. And the guy sitting next to me whispered into a phone as he picked his teeth with his fingernail, wiggling his tongue and sucking in an attempt to free whatever it was.

"So?" the Cyclops said after quite the pause.

"So?" I answered back, attempting to remain unaffected.

The guy who was looking out the window jerked his head toward me and laughed heartily. "Dis fuggin' guy," he said. I seemed to be invisible to the guy who was whispering into his phone.

"So, it's done then," the one eyed guy said.

"Oh yeah," I said. "It's done."

The one eyed guy smiled and sat back, a bit surprised. "No problems then?"

"That depends. Whose problems are you talking about?" I asked.

The one eyed guy guffawed and relit the cigar stub that was sticking out of his mouth as the guy next to him hooted, "Dis fuggin' guy, I tell ya, dis fuggin' guy." The guy next to me began speaking into his phone more urgently, with a cheerier tone.

"And you're okay with it?" the one eyed guy asked as he blew smoke over my head.

"It was fun," I said, which sent the two men before me into a bout of constrained laughter. Even the man sitting next me chuckled into his phone. The guy looking out the window pulled out a pack of smokes and jerked one out, catching it between his lips, and he jerked another out, offering it to me.

"I have my own," I said as I reached under my trench coat and pulled out my mechanical mod with a chimney tank attached to it. I took a long draw and blew out a cloud of vapor like a fog machine. As the vapor dissipated, I saw that the two men had turned to cement. The guy next to me was muted. The one eyed guy slowly and carefully reached forward, took the brim of my trilby between his fingers and lifted it up.

"Who da fugg is dis guy?" the man next to him ejaculated.

"Hold the phone," the guy next to me said and snapped his phone shut, turning in his seat.

"Well, th-th-that's all folks," I joked. I attempted to make a break for it, but I was grabbed and punched in the gut and carried as if on a litter through the crowd as my legs flailed. A door was opened for me and as we came through I was thrown like a steak to a grill onto a sturdy table. As the door shut me in, I rolled over and saw that I was lying on the Ziggy symbol that was engraved deeply into the wood. The door swung open again and in came Phil Zigfield like Frankenstein's monster, big and solid, with a long face that looked like it was made out of limestone, scarred and soulless, with sickeningly yellowed eyes and big teeth biting between thin lips like a skull wearing a mask of flesh.

"Search him," he commanded.

My body was intruded by hands crawling around in my pockets, jabbing at me inside my pants and under my trench coat. They pulled out my vaping items and tossed them onto the table. "Look at this," one of the men said after pulling out the balled up sandwich wrapper. Smokey unwrinkled it and spread it out on the table, smoothing it with his palms.

"Is that Light's handwriting?" he asked.

The men huddled around him. "Could be," one of them said. "What does it say?"

"Pastrami on rye?" I suggested.

Meanwhile more hands intruded and someone said, "Wait, I think we have something here," as he unfolded the paper found in my pants pocket. Now I knew I was doomed. It had Larry Zigfield's photo on it with all his personal information.

"Get him on the phone!" Smokey shouted. "You!"

he roared at me. "What are you, some kind of private dick?"

"How did you get in here?" another guy screamed at me.

"You fugged up, you fugging mutt," my former bar mate said.

Phil was handed a phone. "Was there some little shit thinks he's Dick Tracy snooping around the store today? No? How about pastrami on rye? That ring any bells? Yeah? Well he's got your mug shot in his pocket. No I'm not kidding, we have him right here. Had the gonads to come right in, snooping around. Okay then." Phil pressed a button ending the call and said, "Light don't know this schmuck from Adam. He was snooping around the store this morning."

"Listen fugg face you better start talking," I was shouted at.

"Who do you work for?"

"Don't all talk at once," I said, thinking I still might be able to woo them with my wit.

"Well he's not PD, that's for sure," Phil said.

"Who cares who this schmuck is? Smoke him and dump him. End of story," the one eyed guy said calmly, as if making a sensible proposition that he expected to be taken seriously.

"You gonna talk, heh?"

"Larry's ex-wife put you up to this?"

"The son-a-bitch was sitting right there pretending to be Oswego," the one eyed guy said as if revealing the punch line to a joke that caused everyone in the room to exclaim at once.

"What?" Phil roared, grabbing me by the lapels and pulling me up. "Is that true?"

"Where's Oswego you rat bastard?"

"About sixty miles west of here," I muttered.

"Oh, dis fuggin' guy, dis fuggin' guy."

"Don't say another word," Phil said. "Better we don't know this prick's story. That way if someone comes asking we don't know nothing. Put all his stuff back in his pockets. Don't leave a trace. Take him for a ride and smoke that sucker."

Just then the door opened letting in dance music for a moment and the crowd of thugs surrounding me went silent as they parted like the red sea. A man came walking toward me. He had a pockmarked face that seemed oddly familiar. He entwined his fingers together, cracking his knuckles through his black leather gloves. "I'll take care of this," he said.

"You want to take care of this?" Phil asked.

"I'll take care of this. *Personally*," the man reiterated.

My items were shoved back into my pockets and I was taken by the arms and feet through a door, into a room where I could see cartons upon cartons of name brand cigarettes. A sliding false wall was opened and I found myself in the same storage room where I had been hiding all day. Someone unlocked the back door where a long black Cadillac was waiting, its engine purring and its rear lights glowing red. I could see through the window that the man with the pockmarked face was behind the wheel before the big trunk popped open like a hungry bird and I was thrown in; the hood shut down upon me. And the wheels below me began moving at a slow, steady pace, making corners cautiously and patiently. I squirmed around in the trunk and managed to get an e-cig out and had a vape while I waited for my annihilation. As if to mock the dire situation I was in, the man was playing The Very Best of Dean Martin. Martin's voice was soothing as he sang to whimsical music that frolicked like there wasn't a care in the world. I imagined Martin on a beach, with a flowery garland around his neck, strumming on a banjo of sorts that my mind invented. Then he was in Venice floating down a canal on a gondola singing to the moon, just a dark silhouette against the satellite's glow. Next Martin was wearing a cowboy hat and a shawl as he sat on an old horse that was trotting along. The car stopped for a while with the engine purring as Martin was on a Las Vegas stage, snapping his fingers with the spotlight on him, standing in front of a choir of feathery angels wearing sea shells for bras.

The music stopped midsentence. I heard the driver's door open and shut. Footsteps approached from the side. Keys jingled. There was a click and a pop and the hood came up. The man stood there looking down at me, his hands shoved in his corduroy jacket pockets as I blew a cloud of vapor out into the fresh air.

"You certainly have a set of gonads on you," he said, "I'll give you that." I lifted my head to look around at my surroundings. I assumed I'd be in an isolated corn field, where I would be forced to dig my own grave, after which I'd promptly have a bullet put in my head. But we were in a Chicago back alley. "Come on, get out of there," he said. He stood back, giving me room as I climbed out of the trunk, my legs aching with cramps. I sat on the bumper, waiting for instructions. "Get your hat," he said. His words took a moment to sink in before I looked back and found my trilby in the trunk. "You need to talk to Vera before you go any further," he said.

"So, you're her Inside Man," I murmured.

"Don't come to the hideout like that," he whined. "What were you thinking? What was your plan? Do you even have a plan?" he asked as he put a ziggy to his mouth and lit it. I took a drag off my e-cig. In unison we blew clouds at each other. Then the Inside Man walked to the driver's door and got in the Cadillac. Dean Martin began right where he left off. *You're Nobody, Til Somebody, Loves Yooou.* I slammed his trunk closed for him as he pulled away.

Oh, Yugo, forgive me, but I must cut this letter short. As you can imagine, the experience was profoundly horrifying and in order to write it out like this, I had to relive it. I must relax now and have a vape. I will write again soon. I promise.

XOXO
Your One and Only Melvin

Exhibit 27

Fire damaged ticket stub
discovered at the Englewood Library.
Used as a bookmark in a copy of
A History of American Tobacco Plantations by B. Saul Bubb.

THIRD WRAP: Coil Pop

Dear Yugo,

Much has happened since last I wrote. I presently fear for the future of humanity. This has nothing to do with what I've been telling you about Vera Grimmel and the Ziggies. That is water under the bridge. I got mixed up with some gothics, you see, who convinced me to let them use my e-juice lab to hold a séance with a Ouija board. I discovered too late that they had successful conjured up a legion of elemental spirits, perhaps even demons, that became trapped within the bottles of e-juice inside a crate that the séance leader was sitting on, like so many genies waiting to be freed. I say too late because some of these bottles of juice were shipped out the next day to customers. It has come to my attention that when these inter-dimensional forces are vaped, horrific bouts of possession take place. I have a list of people who received one of these haunted bottles and am seriously considering tracking each of them down to perform exorcisms on them.

This has nothing to do with you, so I will spare you the gory details, but if my handwriting is shaky and hard to read, just know that I have not been this paranoid since that morning when I sent you adrift in the dinghy onto Lake Michigan. Please trust me when I say I tried in vain to use my Cuisinart 5-speed hand mixer as a makeshift motor to set you off in the right direction, but it became tangled in some sea weed and, struggling with it, I lost balance and fell forward into the water. Off you went in a straight line away from me, at a considerable speed from the weight of my struggle. I can't imagine the fear you must have felt when you woke to find yourself abandoned like that.

What you felt must have been similar to what I felt when I was locked in the trunk of the Inside Man's Cadillac, believing I would soon be placed face down in a field; but just as someone must have come to your rescue, I too was set free, in an alley that happened to be not three blocks from the motel on Lincoln Avenue where Vera Grimmel was staying.

I made haste and jimmied the lock with some ribbon wire and a Totally Wicked referral card. Only a sliver of dull streetlamp broke through the pulled curtains as I stood in her room. In front of me lie Vera, with her covers pulled up to her chin, flat on her back, both her feet pointed straight up in red slippers, snoring away like a hacksaw. I silently took the only chair and lifted it to the side of her bed and sat on it, then put my carto tank to my mouth and had a vape. The light from my battery and the sizzling sound startled her. She jolted, pulling the covers up to her nose, staring at me wide eyed.

"It's me," I said. "It's Melvin Provario."

"Melvin," she gasped. "Crap you took the piss out of me. What are you . . . how did you . . . I figured I'd never see *you* again."

"Yet here I am," I said. "I wanted you to know, I haven't made a decision yet."

"You could have picked up the phone for that," she said hoarsely.

"What makes you think I'm capable of murder?" I asked. "Why *me*? Why not hire a professional?"

"Hire a professional?" she scoffed. "How? Look in the phonebook?" She slid herself up the headboard and huffed. "Let's say I find someone, let's assume he's not the fuzz. Let's say he comes highly recommended by someone I know. He's going to leave a trail of breadcrumbs right to me. In a situation like this, it's best to deal with a complete stranger with no ties to me and no ties to anyone I know. Nobody would suspect a person like that."

"You said one of my customers recommended me," I pried.

"That was just someone I met in a bar. I didn't give her details and she never saw me again. There's nothing tying her to me, nothing tying you to to to the, the — "

"To the victims?" I asked.

"Victims? That's not how I would describe them," she objected.

"That's my problem," I said. "No matter how I spin it, I see them as victims."

"Then why are you here?" she spat angrily. "Do you mind?" she said, reaching for the lamp.

"Go ahead," I said, taking a vape.

The lamp went on. She was wearing her white gloves. She reached back and fluffed her pillow against the headboard and sunk into it. Her thick makeup was horribly unrefined, as if applied in a rush, with a thick glob of foundation stuck in her cleft like a scab. A clown couldn't put on more makeup than this, I thought, and she read my mind. "I have psoriasis," she explained hastily. "I look like a cantaloupe with cauliflower for hands," and before I could grill further she changed the subject. "Let's begin again, Mr. Provario. Why do I have the pleasure of your company this evening?"

"You've planted this seed in my mind." I tapped my forehead with my pointer, brushing the brim of my trilby with my knuckle. "Your proposal has been ticking like a time bomb in me. I couldn't stop it from ticking so I went to meet Larry to see if I could at least defuse it."

"You met Larry Zigfield?" she quizzed, sliding up farther against the headboard with interest.

"He seemed to be a nice enough guy," I said.

"Oh, don't be fooled," she said with contempt. "He's a vile, cruel person."

"And then I met Phil."

"You met Smokey?" she gasped, spreading her fingers on the chest of her nightgown. "No you didn't."

"Yes. I did. I was in the hideout, in the meeting room. It was exactly as you described it."

"You were in the meeting room, with Phil Zigfield," she stated with skepticism. "I doubt that very much."

"Why is that, Vera?"

"Because you're not buried six feet in a hole," she said defiantly.

I let out one single "Ha!" and then had a vape. "I was nearly in that hole—would have been, too, if not for divine intervention. I think you know who I'm talking about."

"Perhaps it would be best not to talk about *him*," she said.

"You talk about breadcrumb trails? Isn't your Inside Man made out of bread?"

"There's no such thing as a perfect plan, Melvin," she quibbled. "Sure, I have my source. Right now you of all people should be thankful for that."

"You know what I think?" I said. "I think it was sheer luck that your source was there to bail me out. You know what I think?" and I reached over and swiped my arm across the dresser, sending a little coffee machine flying across the room; it shattered into pieces as it hit the wall. "I think I came this close," and I leaned forward and stuck the tiny space between my thumb and finger into her face as she flinched, "this close to dying tonight!"

"How's that my fault?" she cried out.

"Because you planted the seed," I shrieked. "And now, after tonight—"

"Wait, you were there *tonight*?"

"Yeah, tonight. The son of a bridge dropped me off in an alley not three blocks from here. He *knew* what he was doing."

She sat up straight and adjusted her wig. "Are you sure you weren't followed?"

"Well, gee, I don't know, Vera. You came to me. You must have at least some confidence in my abilities."

"I never told you to stroll right in there like some lost little lamb. Those guys are dangerous. If you're going to do it—do it right. Let me help you."

I sat back in the chair, had a vape and then crossed one leg over the other. "Come out with it, Vera. Let's have it. What exactly happened to your brother Patty?"

Vera seemed flustered, legitimately surprised by the question. She adjusted her breasts under the cover, and then she stared at the space in front of her for a moment, contemplating something, and gave me what seemed to be an involuntary nod of her head, before she began speaking, slowly, as if speaking to a patch of fog. As Vera spoke, I could see one of her false eyelashes loosening every time she blinked, until at some point it was gone, having fallen away unnoticed during her narrative.

"It all started with one single cigarette. It wasn't Patty's fault. You see, he suffered from, he suffered from" and she balled up her hand and coughed into it and then started with her annoying, rapid stuttering. "Ahahbaba-cacadade." I sighed impatiently. "Didie? Dodow?"

"Down syndrome!"

"Yes! Yes!" she said as she cleared her throat. She

leaned over and gave me a single pat on my knee. "Exactly!

"He used to hang out at Ziggy Light's and he wasn't a bother. Sometimes Larry would let him sweep the floor for a bowl of coleslaw. Oh how he loved coleslaw. So one day some bum comes in asking Larry if he could buy a single. Larry says he don't sell singles. But Danny Zigfield happens to be there, sitting on a stool near the deli with a face like a comic strip, and he says, 'I'll sell you a ziggy,' and he pulls out a phony pack of Marlboro's and hands the bum a square in exchange for seventy-five cents. Patty, who had this habit of mimicking people, with his eyes peering through his thick glasses and his tongue protruding from his missing teeth, he says, 'I want a single too,' and Danny gives him a single, inserts it behind his ear, and then asks for the seventy-five cents. 'I don't have it,' Danny admits and some mutt behind the counter laughs and says, 'Dis fuggin guy.'

"'That's okay Captain Retardo,' Danny says, 'I know you're good for it. But don't forget, you owe me.'

"'I owe you,' Patty says and claps his hands.

"'So're you gonna smoke it or what,' says the mutt.

"'Yeah. Put it in your mouth and smoke it,' Danny insists and Patty fumbles with the ziggy and puts it in his mouth backwards and Danny lights the filter end and it catches fire and burns black with an awful stink and they laugh. But Larry's not laughing. He's already thinking the retard could be a liability, and he tells them to get the hell out of his joint.

"Danny's joke on Patty wasn't over. The next time he sees him walking down the street he stops him. It was Danny and a few of his wigger friends, that's right, *they* stop him," she paused to interpret my gesture and then she continued. "Wiggers. Real white trash who

100

like to ink their apathy onto their faces. 'You have my money?' Danny asks and Patty searches through his pockets pulling out pennies and nickels and holds out a handful for Danny who says, 'What's this?'

"'Seventy-five cents,' Patty says.

"'You forgot the interest,' Danny says. 'Now you owe me a buck fifty.' Patty's eyes are flinching behind his thick glasses, because the wiggers start poking at him and nudging him and then one of them slaps his hand and all the change goes flying into the air out onto the street, some of it going down a sewer drain. 'Look what you did,' Danny says. 'I'll tell you what. I'll make a bet with you. If you win you owe me nothing, but if I win you owe me double.'

"'Okay.'

"'You have to say the following sentence five times without making a mistake,' Danny says.

"'Okay.'

"'Mrs. Puggy Wuggy has a square cut punt.'

"'Mrs. Piggly Wiggly.'

"'No. Mrs. *Puggy Wuggy* has a square cut punt.'

"'Mrs. Puggy Wuggy.'

"'Has a square cut punt.'

"'Has a sqawr cunt put.'

"'What did you say?' And they laugh.

"So Patty agrees, he owes Danny three dollars. And these games, these games go on and on until Danny claims Patty owes him *three hundred* dollars. One day the heat is on and Danny's too afraid to drive the shipment of hijacked tobacco over to his brother Roger's shop, so he's sitting there in Ziggy Light's and he says to Larry, 'Let Captain Retardo drive it,' and Larry asks him if he's crazy and Danny says no, besides, 'Captain Retardo owes me three hundred dollars, don't you Captain Retardo,' and Patty nods his head up and down, proud to be indebted to Danny.

"Larry asks, 'Do you at least know how to drive?' and Patty nods his head and he puts his hands up as if steering an invisible wheel while making motor sounds with his lips and tongue.

"To make a long story short, Melvin, Patty crashes the van into a light pole and the contraband gets discovered and, see, now Patty owes the Ziggies thirty thousand dollars, but he doesn't know it. He thinks he's one of them, draws the Ziggy logo with a marker on his hand and starts bragging to people. He works for the Ziggies, he claims, he *is* a Ziggy in fact. And the Ziggies, they let him slide for a while, and Smokey gives Danny quite the slapping around as a matter of fact, for instigating the entire mess, and Larry swears up and down he knew from the start, the retard was going to be a liability

"But, you see," and Vera shook her head grimly, "one day Phil is sitting at the booth in Smokey's with one of the most notorious gangsters in Chicago, hashing out the details of distributing ziggies to a chain of stores that he shakes down, when the gangster, he says, 'To be honest, Smokey, I don't know how I can trust your operation,' and Phil, offended, demands an explanation" (Vera was getting excited like a child remembering the details of an extravagant fairy tale) "and the gangster lets him know there's some retard walking around claiming he's part of the family, that word out on the street is this retard turned over a shipment to the cops and probably sang too, but Smokey, he didn't do *nothing* about it, even lets the guy run around sporting Ziggy ink. 'So how can I trust an operation like that?' the gangster asks.

"Smokey assures the gangster that he plans to do something about this problem, and just so there's no mistaking his resolve, he invites a couple of the gangster's goons along for the ride that night," and as Vera began sniffling, I handed her a wad of organic cotton balls from CVS, "when they snatch my brother Patty, and put him in the trunk of Roger's car, and drive him to a big old abandoned factory," and she paused to wipe away her tears, black with mascara, "and strip off his clothes and tie him up, and burn him all over his body with ziggies," and she blew some snot into the cotton, "and all five brothers are there, I swear, all five of them, Melvin, all five. Just to put the sight of it into the goons, who they know will report back what they see to the gangster, Bart pulls himself out and urinates in Patty's mouth, and as he's choking on it, Danny jams a lit ziggy into Patty's eyeball, and then he relights it, slowly and deliberately, before jamming it into the other eyeball; and Larry, Larry is there, I swear. Larry takes Patty's little pecker and snips it off with a cigar cutter and shoves it into Patty's mouth as the poor man child screams for help, and as the bloody little tip of flesh sticks out between his lips, Larry tries to light the end of it with his gold lighter and they laugh and yell at him to smoke it; and as poor Patty is bleeding out all over the floor, Phil puts a rubber tire around his body and drenches it with gasoline and he lights it on fire, and poor poor Patty is taking too long to die, rolling around and screaming, so Roger gets into his Chrysler and—"

"Stop!" I shouted. "I can't bear to hear any more." I felt so nauseated I couldn't even keep down a vape. "I will never be able to unhear that story," I said. "Now you've haunted me with that! Now what am I supposed to do?"

"Start with Bart," she whispered to me through her clenched teeth. "He's come out of the hospice for the second god damned time and is back in intensive care. He refuses to die."

My lovely Yugo, with all the horror going on last October, I fell into a gloom that I had a hard time snapping out of. Brandon recognized my depression, saying I was so down that I wasn't even vaping with gusto, so he took it upon himself to force me to follow him around in an attempt to cheer me up. I sat through one of his Samurai classes. The topic of the day was how to properly bow. Brandon and the rest of the class spent the hour wearing robes with sticks through their hair, bowing in front of mirrors. "I am from Chicago of the Bieberman family! Huh!! If there is a brave man amongst you, fight your duel!" Despite the monotony, the company started lifting my spirits, so I agreed to go with Brandon to boy band practice in the parking lot of the McDonald's Xpress and although it took me a while to get the hang of it, once I shed myself of my trench coat, I really started to get some moves myself. They call themselves *The New Nature Degrees* and they aren't half bad. Afterward, they decided to go to the Laundromat to try to hit it off with the women who go there wearing nothing but their pajamas, but I had a date with Elle so we parted ways for the evening.

Elle also did a fine job cheering me up last autumn. She challenged me to a game of who can wrap a parallel subcoil the fastest, with extra points given for lack of hot spots and perfect ohms. It was a tie. We then attached our atomizers to a dueling juice mod and sipped vapor like two love birds with straws going into the same strawberry float.

Eventually, Elle pried it out of me, the whole story, and my fear and self-loathing vanished with one punch on my shoulder. I'm telling you, Elle whacked me good and hard. "What are you moping about Skippy? It sounds to me like this witch owes you a ton of money. Are you telling me she hasn't coughed up one cent yet? No? Then you're going to demand some of it before you even think about finishing the job." It wasn't a suggestion; it was a command. For the second time, Elle agreed to be my partner in crime, and even though this time it involved something much, much more serious than stealing a gold plated mod, Elle acted like it was nothing but a thing and encouraged me to set up another meeting with Vera to hash out the final details of the sordid affair. "She can't exactly put it in writing, but she'll have a hard time weaseling out of it if she knows her secret won't be safe with *me*."

The meeting was set for 6 PM at a diner that was part of a motel that was four motels down from the motel where Vera was staying. Elle and I decided to make a day of it. Before meeting Vera we would take a ride farther north to check on Granmama, and when Elle showed up on schedule that afternoon at the Subway shop, I was delighted to find that she had freshly dyed her hair white (not by any means blonde, mind you, but pure white) and she was wearing some little tight denim shorts and a purple tube top that was in width perhaps three quarters of the length of my hand, with her ribcage underneath as if there were a pair of wings beneath her flesh, with such a tiny navel that I doubted the tip of my pinky would fit into it. She jumped up and wrapped her arm around my neck and gave me a wet kiss on the cheek, and I may have unknowingly been in hell, Yugo, but it felt like I was in heaven. As it turned out, Elle wasn't in the same state of bliss that I was in, as I will explain in due time. At first I felt the revelation about Elle was karmic payback for how Danny Zigfield was led along, but as the truth unfurled, I've come to believe there were other factors at play.

You see, it turned out Danny was quite gay. As usual, Vera knew everything and instructed Mr. Vape on how to seduce him to get close enough to kill him. She knew of a gay chat room he hung out in and she instructed Mr. Vape on some of Danny's likes and dislikes. She gave him a laptop that he carried around, so he could hold conversations with Danny whenever he found a hotspot and found him online. They chatted a lot about *anoblazing* and although he had no idea what anoblazing was, he didn't want to appear ignorant, so Mr. Vape let on that he was *really* into it.

It came to be, after about a week of flirtation, that Danny and Mr. Vape would go on a date, to Wiggerfest, scheduled to be held in an abandoned drive-in theater on the outskirts of Earlville. Danny would be taking a train out to the city to attend Bart's memorial on that day anyway, so Mr. Vape offered to pick him up and they would go to the fest together, and Mr. Vape would leave him off afterward in Joliet on his way back to Chicago. He picked him up in the Camry that he borrowed from Uncle Nick's secret lot, and was a bit miffed when he found himself engaged in a rather lengthy conversation with Danny comparing and contrasting Dostoyevsky to David Sedaris on the long ride out, but he went with the flow. The drive-in actually served as the parking lot and vendor area for the fest, and the actual band lineup would play in a huge field that was a walk away, giving Danny and Mr. Vape some more time to get to know each other before being overwhelmed with horrorcore music headlined by Bang Blast Ya Head Off featuring Twisted Fupped Uck Hustla. Mr. Vape was pleased when some clowns in the parking lot tried to sell Danny a dub sack and he ignored them. Instead of getting high, he dragged a ziggy (counterfeit Winston, the brand I use to smoke) and Mr. Vape puffed on an Aspire CE5 clearomizer on a box mod, and everything was okay.

Mr. Vape wasn't sure what all the tattoos on Danny's face were supposed to mean: above his eyebrows were some type of cat claws; three smiley faces were on his chin; some cursive writing that Mr. Vape wasn't brave enough to stare at long enough to decipher were over the bags under his eyes; and he had a series of what appeared to be fluttering moths for a mustache; and there was a pyramid, like from the back of a dollar bill, centered on his forehead with a beam of light, like a transporter beam from a flying saucer, coming down from it over his nose. These were just the few that Mr. Vape could make out as he glanced at him from time to time; they existed amidst a collage of dots and exes and hieroglyphics that continued over his freshly shaven scalp.

Danny was missing one of his upper teeth, the second one to the right of center, obvious every time he smiled. And he had dark brown eyes that were sunken in and looked oblivious and happy and sad and confused all at the same time. He seemed very gentle and unashamed as he took Mr. Vape's hand in his, as they walked toward the bandstand; and surprisingly Mr. Vape didn't feel embarrassed walking hand in hand with him, because in his simple t-shirt, blue jeans and sneakers, it wasn't all that clear whether Danny was male or female; and I suppose the same could have been said about Mr. Vape, his body hidden beneath his trench coat and the top of his face shadowed by his trilby. By the look of the crowd, Wiggerfest was going to be a virtual freak show, so who cared?

Mr. Vape found the concert not in the least displeasing. At that time he was obsessing on an old cassette tape of The Blue Nile, playing it over and over, each time finding himself caught up in an hypnotic spell that put him to sleep, causing the final songs to be mere parts of a blurred opium dream—so this loud, rude, crude white boy rapping set to hardcore guitar and eerie synthesizer was refreshingly awakening. On stage it was a carnival of oddities, a circus of body piercing and face paint, and although the audience was composed of baseball cap sporting wild people who looked like they all just got released from county, no major trouble ensued and everyone had a good time. The lack of unrest didn't stop the state police from surrounding the farm at the end of the show, with all their cop car lights flashing blue, as men and women in ranger hats with giant flashlights directed traffic out of Earlville as abruptly and swiftly as possible; but even that went smoothly. As Mr. Vape pulled up through a dark, nearly abandoned side street of Joliet, to Danny's tiny frame house, Danny invited Mr. Vape inside.

So far; so good.

The plan was to tempt Danny to try his e-juice and when he started getting into it, to switch the juice to a deadly concentrate of nicotine, which Mr. Vape wasn't sure would kill him, but would certainly knock him on his ass and incapacitate him long enough for Mr. Vape to get the black bag from the trunk of the Camry to do the dirty deed. But Danny ended up throwing him for a loop when he asked him to make himself at home, which he did, on an aged sofa, and Danny went into the other room to get more comfortable. When he came back a short time later, he was completely naked, a tattooed sphere on a hairless, pink body. He sat on a reclining chair across from Mr. Vape, lit a counterfeit Winston, spread his legs over the armrests, and hunched up using one of his arms to spread his leg out even farther. Mr. Vape sat there stunned, face to face with Danny's rust colored anus. Danny moistened his finger in his mouth and massaged the opening as if applying lipstick then proceeded to reach down between himself to insert the filter end of his ziggy. It glowed orange, and as he pulled it away as naturally as one would from lips at a cocktail party, a stream of smoke came puffing out.

Mr. Vape assumed anoblazing was some type of homosexual act, and he wasn't worried about it, since he didn't plan to let Danny get that far; but now it made perfect sense why Danny kept talking about smoking, why he was so curious when Mr. Vape told him that he doesn't smoke, he vapes. *Danny had never seen a vaper anoblaze before!* He thought that meant someone who vapes *after* sex, but the dots were all connected now. Danny expected him to have a vape with his asshole. This was *not* something that Vera warned him about.

Mr. Vape saw no way to get out of it. If he was going to cozy up to Danny enough to gain his trust, he would need to do it. If he didn't, he'd be exposed as the fraud he was. If he acted in any way like he didn't know what he was doing or needed some assistance or was reluctant, he'd be given away; and then he might see the not so kind side of Danny Zigfield.

As Mr. Vape began undressing, theatrically, as if doing a strip tease, Danny was delighted, relaxed and chuckling. Mr. Vape felt a rush of dread. What if he was unable to pull off a reverse fart? If no vapor came out of his ass, he'd be caught just the same. Knowing he had no way out of it but to at least try, he plopped down completely naked on the sofa and groped into one of his trench coat pockets for a tank. He wrapped his arm around his two legs and pulled his knees toward his face and plunged the drip tip in, straining his muscles, trying desperately to suck with his anus; and then he heard the atomizer sizzle. He let it sizzle until the ten second automatic battery shut off kicked in, and as the light started blinking between his hairy cheeks, he pulled the drip tip out, but he saw no vapor. Danny started looking at him, first curiously, then suspiciously, and then his eyes seemed to fill with angry enlightenment, until Mr. Vape managed to blow like a table leg being dragged across a hardwood floor, ejaculating a thick white cloud of vapor that expanded and saturated the parlor. Danny sat back and laughed until tears came out of his eyes, and then he enjoyed another anoblaze off his ziggy.

Mr. Vape knew he was in trouble. His intestines quivered involuntarily and his vision became blurry. *No, I didn't*, he told himself, but when he looked at the tank that was still in his hand, it was, *Oooh boy, yes, I did*. In his haste to get it over with, he had retrieved the wrong tank from his coat and had anovaped the deadly nicotine concentrate. I'm not sure what happened next, my dear Yugo, but I imagine Mr. Vape's eyes rolled up inside of his head as he went temporarily comatose.

He woke in Danny's bed hearing birds chirping. He could smell aromatic coffee brewing. His head actually felt pretty good, like his nicotine craving had been satisfied for a week, but the rest of his body, well, not so much. I don't want to go into details, my sweet, but it was obvious that Danny had his way with him. I suppose I can't call it date rape, since he didn't slip Mr. Vape any drugs, but that didn't ease the growing rage bubbling inside of him. He came out of the bedroom into the parlor to find his clothes still piled on the sofa. He could see through a doorway that Danny was in the kitchen, preparing breakfast on the stove. Mr. Vape got dressed and went out the screen door to the Camry to retrieve the black bag from the trunk. And he sat on Danny's sofa waiting.

Now he had more than one reason to do it. Do it for Patty. Do it for the money. Do it to shut Danny up so he couldn't tell anyone about what happened.

Danny came out of the kitchen in a long bathrobe tied loosely around his waist, carrying a bamboo breakfast tray made up lovingly with a plate of bacon and waffles and potatoes and coffee. Mr. Vape reached his hands into his trench coat pockets. "I hope you like it, Darling," Danny said as he gently bowed to place the tray over his lap. Mr. Vape sprung like a cat, whipping out two personal vaping devices, each with a long bent top drip tip, and he plunged them into eyes that popped like peanut shells. The tray of food came flipping all over Mr. Vape as Danny fell back with a squeal, his clawed hands groping at his face. Mr. Vape pulled the sock filled with Sony 18650s out of his bag and he lunged forward, whacking him on the head with a crack. He went to the floor with a thud. Mr. Vape quickly shoved a stack of Japanese cotton pads into Danny's mouth and then went to work with the 20 gauge kanthal wire.

By the time he came to, moaning and trying to cough through the cotton, blinded and completely confused, Mr. Vape had Danny wrapped head to foot with kanthal and even remembered to stick a penny in the fuse box so that it wouldn't blow. He had doused his naked body with a 100 milliliter bottle of some horrible key lime pie flavored e-juice that he got on sale that tasted like nothing but burnt pie crust. "I knew I'd find a use for this stuff someday," he cackled. Mr. Vape wired the two ends of the kanthal to the positive and negative posts of the MP Mega-Vape that I had invented and he plugged it into the outlet.

"Let's have a vape," he said and flicked the switch. The kanthal began glowing orange, one wrap at a time, from the center outward, sizzling its way over Danny's crotch and thighs, down his legs and up his torso, all the while blowing massive vapor that had a pie crust and burning flesh stench to it. Danny struggled like an earthworm with muffled screams. "Talk about a macrocoil," Mr. Vape cheered, as the hundred wrap coil glowed bright orange. "Twenty-five hundred ohms. Perfect."

Mr. Vape came through the screen door, the vapor from Danny-the-wick pouring out of the house into the morning air. He got into the Camry and pulled out his mod to have a vape but discovered the drip tip was missing. That wasn't good. It meant that it was still lodged in Danny's eye socket. He thought about going back in for it, but he had to get out of there. The rug underneath Danny would surely catch fire soon. He took out his other mod and attempted to have a vape, but the drip tip was clogged, so he pulled it off the tank and blew through it and out came some of Danny's eyeball like toothpaste.

I was concerned about how scantily Elle was dressed, but at the same time, I saw in it possibilities. It was true that though the day was sunny, even hot for the season, especially for me under my trench coat, the truth was the evenings were growing quite chilly. At the back of my mind, however, this suggested Elle may eventually snuggle up underneath my coat like a little bird, and the notion of such closeness, such an opportunity to express tenderness, made my heart flutter. So I stayed silent on the matter. In my mind we were going to end up on the beach, the sun setting behind the skyscrapers, a little fire burning down to kindling in front of us, as Elle and I cuddled to stay warm. This was preposterous, of course, since our destination would take us about as far away from the lake as possible and, also, it's illegal to build fires on the beach, but the fantasy was soothing as we rode the el train to the far northwest side.

Elle sat across from me and, as usual, we played our secret games. That time it was stealth vaping while mocking another person on the train. Elle bloated up her face to represent the overweight woman at the far end of the car, vaping off her Lemo on her iStick, blowing the vapor behind her seat. I stuck my nose up and tried to act all proper, representing the rich couple who seemed to be made out of plastic, as I vaped off my Sigelei 100 with a Russian 91%, blowing the vapor into a coat pocket. Our game was interrupted when Elle's tight little shorts started vibrating. She pulled a phone out of her pocket and had a quiet conversation that bewildered me. I had never seen Elle with that particular phone before and wondered why she was being so secretive, but I didn't want to seem like an overburdening boyfriend, so I didn't pry.

Elle came up with what I thought was a really nifty idea. Since we were heading up in that direction anyway, we should stop at a certain vape shop that she knew of, called ZestyD's. I heehawed, letting her know that I was familiar with that shop, and I told her a funny anecdote about it. I had been frequenting an online forum called Vape Mania when a quite nasty tit for tat developed between me and some user named ZestyD. As is common in these situations, the mind's eye tends to paint a picture of the anonymous adversary, and more often than not this picture is inaccurate. One time when I was trolling CNN someone insisted that I was an overweight, self-loathing middle aged woman, and when I tried to correct the notion the person would have none of it, insisting he knew exactly what I was and asking why I was denying it. Anyhow, my picture of ZestyD was that of a redneck bully who worked in an auto shop by day, who had grease under his fingernails and who, by night, liked to pretend online that he was an expert at essential oils. We argued with each other, taunted each other through private messages, and played mind games on each other, usually resulting in the thread getting shut down by a moderator. Well, as reality insisted, I would one day stumble into the very vape shop Elle wanted to visit, only to discover ZestyD was a short, plump woman with thick glasses and a smile like the Cheshire Cat, who turned out to be very friendly and whose struggling business inspired sympathy. So sure, I'd love to go to ZestyD's Vape Shop and say hello to my little vape. The expression on Elle's face showed that she found my Scarface impersonation rather irrelevant but she soon enough shook that off and we were back to our stealth vaping game.

In order to get to ZestyD's, we transferred onto a bus at the el station and as the bus passed the vape shop we knew something was up. There were cop cars in front of it and a board up company was already beginning to install some plywood over one of the plate glass windows. We came off the bus and cautiously approached the sidewalk still covered with shattered glass. I don't know why they had strung police tape, because one of the cops lifted it up for us as we entered.

ZestyD was frazzled but trying to maintain her cool as she saw us. She called out, "Don't worry, we're still open for business." Someone had ransacked the place, smashed out the glass display counters, scattered her products all over the place, took a knife to the plush furniture in her little vaping den, pulling out the feathers and polyester stuffing, and spray painted a big Z with a cigarette crossing through it on the wall. I stood in the middle of the room eyeballing the graffiti.

"Those sons of bridges," Mr. Vape cursed. "Does nothing stop those attyholes?"

"Are you sure nothing was stolen?" a female police officer asked as she scrawled in a little book.

ZestyD seemed to be coming out of shock. As she was registering the police officer's question, she looked at me, trying to recognize me. "No," she said drearily as her eyes squinted at me, "it seems they didn't take anything. They just vandalized the place."

I turned to see Elle with thick gloves on, wearing a surgical mask over her nose and mouth, working a big push broom around, sweeping glass and trash into a heap, once in a while springing down to retrieve a mod or an RBA. "Don't just stand there," she called to me, her eye slits trying to give me some code that I didn't understand. "Grab a broom." I started to approach ZestyD to see what she needed me to do but I was accosted by a police officer, who put his hands into my armpits and coaxed my hands above my head. He began to pat me down from neck to ankles. "Any weapons? Any needles?" he asked as he worked my trouser legs.

"No, sir," I said.

"Does this belong to you?" he said as he pulled a personal vaping device out of a pocket.

"Yes, sir," I said.

"I'm not talking to you," he said.

ZestyD shook her head, indicating it wasn't an item from her shop.

"How about this one?" he asked after pulling out a mod. "This one? This one? This one?" ZestyD shook her head.

"Are you the one who's been sleeping in the dumpster behind the Portage?"

"No sir," I said.

"Lift your hat." I pinched my hat and lifted it, letting him see the burn scar that runs from my ear to my temple like SpaghettiOs.

"It's okay, officer," ZestyD said, "I know him."

The officer frowned and then disappeared through the frame of the shattered glass door like a piece of paper caught in the wind.

"What happened?" I asked.

"What happened??" ZestyD laughed, looking around and flinging her hands this way and that.

"Do you need some help?"

"That's a stupid question!" Elle barked at me as she swept some debris out of one of the broken cases into a dustpan with a whisk broom.

I looked up again at the graffiti on the wall and didn't know what I could say. I couldn't after all tell ZestyD that I knew who did it, couldn't tell her that the Ziggies were still in operation even after losing four Zig leaders. Just the notion that I was familiar with the Ziggies would implicate me in what had to be a very puzzling series of deaths. Instead, what came out of my mouth was, "Got any contractor bags?"

Whatever regret I had for what I did to Larry Zigfield vanished at that moment. What I did may have been cruel, but how cruel was it to shatter a young lady's livelihood like that? My dear Yugo, let me go back a week and touch upon that for a moment, when I was hiding in the attic for days at a time.

If I was going to plot the murder of Larry, I needed to get out of there, because if I didn't, I would eventually have to face Brandon who would surely want to kill me. I had received my vape mail for the day, a package from ChopChopTech, a Chinese supplier of ridiculously cheap electronic equipment. I had purchased a Vision Spinner "Style" lithium e-cig battery for half the price of what an authentic Spinner would cost, with free worldwide shipping. It took weeks to get there but it was finally in my hand. It was a real beaut, like a four inch long bullet casing with a 510 ego connector and a variable voltage spin dial that could be adjusted from 3.3 to 4.8 volts; and it had a button with a white LED light inside of it that you could click five times to either turn the battery on or off or just push to have a vape for ten seconds. I should have known something was wrong with it because it was supposed to be 1600 mah but died on me after only two hours of vaping. I used a charger from some other ChopChopTech gadget to plug it into the USB port of the laptop that Vera had given me.

The battery was charging for about an hour. I was at my work table wearing my jeweler's lighted high-power magnifying visor, trying to fine tune the MP-FUK-ALL that had malfunctioned like a flame thrower instead of the guts of an e-hookah, when I noticed something that smelled like burnt marshmallows. I took my visor off and looked at my futon mattress where my battery was charging and I could see that it was having a catastrophic failure, dripping fluid off the side of the bed. I rushed over to unscrew it when a searing hot, blinding light came from it, like a magnesium sparkler, as hot as a welding torch, then it started sparking like a fountain firework. Then kablooey. I shielded my face as its dial shot off at me, followed by a streak of flame, hot oil striking my hands. There was a bang as loud as a gun and the spinner flashed through the air like a missile, hitting the rafters and dropping into the insulation between two sheets of plywood, leaving my futon mattress and the laptop on fire behind it.

I must say I reacted quite swiftly. First I rolled up my burning mattress with the laptop in it and rushed to the little front window like someone with a battering ram and smashed it through, the entire window, glass and wood, falling out with it. The futon fell down one story and landed on the roof of the front porch and luckily it only scorched a few shingles before it slid off and landed in the front yard with huge puffs of black smoke. Then I rushed to the area where the battery was still burning in the insulation and I stomped my foot down to extinguish it but my foot went straight through the drywall and the sparkling battery fell below with a kerplunk. I rushed downstairs and searched in a panic and found it in the bathroom. It landed in the toilet bowl, which was good, but now there was a hole shaped like my foot in the bathroom ceiling.

I left Brandon a note explaining that I had purchased a knock-off that didn't have overcharge protection and I didn't use the correct charger and I apologized and promised to pay for everything when my settlement check arrived and then I got out of there so that I wouldn't have to face him. He was already upset that morning, pacing around crying, "Someone jacked my bike!"

"So how would you do it?" I asked Mr. Vape as I hid in a cubbyhole I had discovered, a narrow, pitch black space between the thrift store and the Hong Kong Express.

"I'd do what Vera suggests. Get to the roof and remove one of the vents to gain access."

"Removing the vent might not be all that easy. It'll make noise and draw attention."

"Do it in the middle of the night, when nobody's

around."

"And then what? Hide inside the store all night and the next day?"

"No, just get the vent off the first night. Then on the second night, right before closing, creep on up there and sneak in undetected."

Vera had explained that Larry trusted nobody and therefore was always the last one to leave the store at night, always the one to lock-up after everyone else left. Even if he was ruffled up by the string of suspicious coincidences regarding the deaths of his brothers, business would still have to go on, so he would be alone in his liquor store for a brief period of time shortly after midnight.

"Okay, once you get in, then what?"

"The sock full of batteries seemed to have worked well last time."

"And then what?"

"I have it all worked out. I'll roll that son of a bridge up like a big cigar with his own sandwich wrapping paper. But first I'll take some loose tobacco from his back room and throw it in with him and shove a bunch of it in his mouth and jam it in there tight around his neck and face. I'll turn him into a human ziggy. Hahaha. Then I'll put him on that big grill of his with his feet right up against that huge exhaust fan. And when he comes to and is pleading for mercy, I'll light the tobacco and turn the exhaust fan on. It should suck the air through the tube he's in and the tobacco around his face should flare. Hahaha. The human ziggy, burning, inch by inch, down his body. I'll have to think of something witty to say though."

"Don't be a square," I suggested.

Mr Vape laughed. "Smoking kills."

I laughed. "That's a good one. And when he's

halfway finished, say 'I knew you were short, but now you're *a short*.'"

"Eh. That was lame. How about when it burns down to his knees, say, 'Now you're the *butt* of the joke.' Hahaha."

"My idea wasn't lame."

"Yes it was."

I forgot who was saying what for a moment and I noticed some people in the sunlight looking in my direction and realized I had been talking out loud. I started whispering so that nobody would hear me.

"Wait, there's a problem with your plan," I said.

"Nu-uh, it's a good plan," Mr. Vape said.

"No, no, think about it. I know Larry's a small guy and probably wouldn't be much effort to lift, but really? Wrapping him in sandwich paper? That paper is like six inches wide. You'd have to roll him over and over and over. It's not plausible."

"Use his rotisserie spit!"

"What rotisserie spit? Why would he have a rotisserie spit? It's a deli. He makes sandwiches. That's right. He makes sandwiches anyway! He doesn't even have a grill, goof ball. He doesn't even have an exhaust fan. You're not thinking about Ziggy Light's. You're thinking about Hog Heaven."

"Hog Heaven?"

"Yeah numbskull, we ate there yesterday, dummy. Man what a stupid idea!"

"Don't call me stupid."

"Hey, I'm not the one who was planning to murder the owner of Hog Heaven."

"Well if you're so smart then what's your plan?"

"Why does it have to be so complicated?" I cried out. "Just hit him a few more times with the sock full of batteries. Mash his brains in and get out of there."

"You're no fun."

"Shut up!"

"Melvin, is that you?"

I snapped out of the wild delirium I had worked myself into and froze, then whispered out, "No."

"Yes it is. I recognize your voice and you're blowing clouds of vapor into the parking lot."

I cautiously came out from the pitch black cubbyhole, temporarily blinded by the sun. "Oh, you again," I said. "Don't' you know white boy dreads went out in the nineties?"

"Are you okay?" Mike Crow asked. He had a purse slung around his shoulder and was wearing bathing trunks with palms trees on them, a tie dye shirt and puka shells.

"Of course," I said, adjusting my trilby and dusting off my trench coat. "What kind of question is that?"

"Have you decided yet?"

"I'm still thinking on it."

"Melvin, the vaping commission hearing is coming up soon. An exclusive isn't going to be an exclusive if you're all over C-SPAN."

"I keep telling you I'm not testifying at any hearing."

"Look, I got your money right here," he said, fumbling around under his trunks to find the little mesh pocket. He pulled out a wad of wrinkled bills.

"How much is that?" I asked as he counted.

"One hundred eighty four dollars and," and he pinched into the pocket once again and brought out the change, "ninety cents."

"And what happened to three hundred dollars?" I scoffed.

"Look, look. I've got one eighty four ninety. Look. It's yours. For eleven minutes of your time."

"When?"

"When? Now. Here. Take it." He dropped the money into a bowl I made with my hands and then he excitedly rummaged through his purse and produced a camcorder.

"Fine then," I said pocketing the money. "I could use some new stainless steel rope for my genesis anyway. But I'm not showing my face," and I pulled my trilby down to my nose.

And so we had our interview. His questions were mostly about the details of the book called *Vape Mania* that had been endorsed by the Institute for the Preservation of the Institution of Cigarettes, aka IPIC, an anti-vaping organization that managed to obtain my personal diary when it purchased the contents of my UHoard storage locker at auction. IPIC lobbied to get it published, but not before brutally editing it and adding all sorts of pro-cigarette commentary to it. They stuck my name onto it and marketed it and now I'm suing them. Have you read *Vape Mania* yet, my dear Yugo? If so, I'm sure you saw through all the lies. That reminds me, Mike even had some questions about you, but don't be concerned, I remained extremely discreet. He seemed pleased enough with the interview and I felt as though I had made a noble attempt to exonerate myself, for after all, I was not willingly the cause of the Vaporgate scandal, not the cheerleader for the intense university study of e-liquids and vaping devices that had been conducted by one of my former kindergarten students. I had nothing to do with that study that led to the hearings that threatened to destroy the vaping community as we knew it. Mike told me I could find the interview on his website as early as the next day, but I didn't care to see it. I knew what I said.

We were running late so we put off checking on

Granmama to meet Vera instead, finding her in a corner booth isolated from the rest of the diner. Elle and I sat across from her and after introductions, Vera offered her gloved hand and they barely shook the tips of their fingers before we were down to business. We all spoke quietly.

"I was afraid you were getting cold feet," Vera said. "I haven't heard from you in a week. Larry seems to be missing. What can I assume about that?"

"It's been taken care of," I assured her.

She nodded her head, blinking her false eyelashes and peering at me skeptically with lowered brows that were comically penciled onto her forehead. Her demeanor was different than it had been during our previous encounters. She seemed less fragile, less intimidated by me, seemed to be bottling up a certain authority, a power over me that she didn't want to reveal but would if things didn't go her way. There also was some weird vibe between her and Elle. She didn't object to me bringing a stranger along with me, seemed to warm up to her a bit too quickly for my taste. What was on her mind, I wondered. Was she so unconcerned because she planned to have her Inside Man off the two of us after the job was done? Or was she merely relieved that I hadn't disappeared? I realized how little I knew about what was going on in the brain behind that forehead caked with Maybelline.

Elle jumped in and gave a spiel about how, in her understanding, Vera initially promised some of the money up front but that I hadn't seen a penny of it yet, and that before any more promises were fulfilled a down payment should be made for services rendered. I thought she was especially cute since she still had the mods and atomizers that she had pilfered from ZestyD's sagging in her tube top as if she had bionic tumors. Vera was listening, nodding her head the whole time, although her eyes remained on me, as if she was studying me, trying to figure me out. I was doing the same to her. For a brief moment it felt as if we were about to pounce on each other but I won the staring contest and Vera lowered her eyes, twirled her spoon around in her cup of tea. She said, as if to a priest behind the screen in a confessional, "I'm afraid if I give him anything of substance he won't finish the job."

"That's not true, is it Melvin?" Elle said cheerfully.

"The deal is for all of them. If even one of them is left alive, I get nothing. You understand that, don't you? Nothing."

"You understand that, don't you, Melvin?" Elle said, nudging me.

"I took care of the others, didn't I?" I whispered. She may have looked away from me but I hadn't taken my eyes off of her. I felt like pulling that red wig off her head and tossing it in her lap just to show her what Mr. Vape was capable of.

"See, that's the thing," she said, lifting her cup and taking a dainty sip, leaving yet another lipstick mark on its edge. "Larry Zigfield is missing. Nobody knows—"

"I told you I took care of that," I said flippantly.

"How do I know you and Larry aren't teamed up against me?" she asked.

I tsked and puckered my lips and scratched the side of my head, but I saw what she was getting at. Larry was gone without a trace. How could she be sure?

"You did it, right, you—" Elle blurted in.

"Shut up!" I snapped at her. She flinched as if someone had just shot her in the chest. "Are you wearing a wire?"

"No," Vera gasped, "are you?"

"No. And neither is my little chickadee here," I said and Elle flinched again and turned in her chair, glaring at me. "Yeah, see, I'm going to tell you a little story, see, about a guy named Mr. Vape. Mr. Vape, see, he had all these elaborate plans worked out, see, but it didn't work out that way. When he came down through the vent hole he didn't have a chance to sneak and hide and do things right, he just came down like a skydiver without a chute, 'cause this broad he knows, see, this red head who goes by the name of Trouble, she didn't tell him there was nothing down there but a flimsy drop ceiling, no. So he came crashing right through feet first, and he was lucky, see, because he came crashing right on top of this little guy with sideburns who was chopping some onions. And there wasn't no choice but to duke it out right then and there because the little guy knew some kind of judo, and while I'm on it, that's another thing this broad named Trouble didn't mention. But Mr. Vape he had the upper hand because having all that dead weight come slamming down on him stunned the little guy and knocked his glasses off. He managed to flip Mr. Vape over a few times and get in some kicks and chops, but Mr. Vape knew what he was doing, wasn't confused like the little guy, was able to grab objects in that cramped kitchen and fling them like his life depended on it, see, the chopping board, see, a knife, a salad bowl, a bread tray, the step stool, a jar of pickles that exploded into the little man's face like a whale sneezing, until the little guy was on the floor cowering in the fetal position, bleeding from his head with one of his arms clearly broken ."

Elle frowned and sagged like a frog.

"Mr. Vape, he didn't know what to do, see, because he didn't have much piss left after the fight. He was pretty beat to shit himself, so he shouted 'Where's your car keys?'

"'Is that all you want?' the little man cried. 'They're right there. Take them. Take them and go away.'

"Mr. Vape snatched the keys off a hook and then he dragged the little man by the back of his deli coat across the floor. The man shouted out, 'What's this about? Please. Tell me,' but Mr. Vape, yeah, see, he didn't have any time for nonsense because nothing was going as planned and he had no idea what was coming next and that's NOT THE WAY HE LIKES IT. He dragged the little man out the back way to the private parking lot and pressed a button on the key and the trunk of the Volvo popped open and the man saw what was going on and managed to get to his feet and another struggle ensued. But Mr. Vape got ahold of his broken arm and twisted it like a boomerang and shoved the little man into the trunk and slammed it shut. 'I know how you feel, buddy, I've been there,' Mr. Vape shouted as he got in the car, and he calmly drove off.

"Mr. Vape headed east and got on Lake Shore Drive and headed south and got off at North Avenue and headed west. He had no idea where he was going or what he was doing, was just wandering around the city, see, trying to figure it out. Then this sense of urgency overcame him. He wondered what else that batty old broad didn't tell him. Maybe she forgot to mention there was a silent alarm in the store, yeah, just maybe. Maybe he tripped it when he went out the back way. Maybe the coppers arrived to find there had been a struggle, suspected foul play. Yeah! Maybe they were looking for that very Volvo at that very moment. He drove in circles around the river, from Ashland to North to Elston to Division and back to Ashland, zigzagging through the side streets as he went. He couldn't ditch the car. They'd find Larry alive inside of

126

it and he knew he'd never get another chance after that. And then he saw what looked like a narrow dirt road going between some trees toward the river, so he maneuvered into it in hopes of finding a secluded spot, real slow and cautious like, and found himself on what must have been some boat launch that was now just a steep, unkempt stretch of mud that should have been fenced off to avoid an accident. He found himself stuck there on the embankment and when he tried to go backward the tire spun and the car crept forward instead. So he got out, see, had no choice, see, managed to gain his footing, pulled himself up with some tree branches.

"He started thinking. Yeah, the spot was secluded enough and the car was stuck and wasn't going anywhere, so he'd have to do it right there. He'd have to open the trunk and finish the job. But what if the little man leapt at him? How would he fight him? They would both tumble into the river. Mr. Vape pulled out his Aspire Nautilus Adjustable Airflow Tank System filled with Castle Long Reserve that had been steeped in a treated oak barrel, and he had a deep, satisfying vape.

"So. While you were sitting there in your motel room powdering that mug of yours, Mr. Vape was crawling back down through the mud to the car door, was sliding in and turning the key and pressing all the buttons so the windows went down. He put the car in neutral and slammed the door shut and pulled himself back up.

"'What are you doing?' the man in the trunk cried.

"Mr. Vape gave the car a shove with his foot and it started to roll. He stood on the embankment watching, having another vape, as the Volvo crashed into the water. It floated away upright with its tail end sticking

127

out. The man in the trunk banged with his fist and kicked in vain under the hood, shouting, 'Let me out of here!'

"'Naw,' Mr. Vape said. 'I think I'll let you steep for a while.'

"'That was witty,' a voice spoke to him.

"'Thanks. I thought so too.'

"You ever see a car sink my friend? Massive bubbles blow out of the water as it rushes into the open windows and then the car goes down. For a while it drifts downstream, the trunk section bobbing as it stubbornly pokes out of the water. Mr. Vape could still hear Larry pounding and crying out, until there were some more bubbles, see, and kablurgle, the car was gone.

"That's my story and I'm sticking to it, see. And, by the way, Mr. Vape left a little message for whoever it may concern. It says if some red headed broad named Trouble doubts it, she can jump into the North Branch of the Chicago River and have a look and see for herself."

I never heard anyone gulp as loudly as Elle did as she sat beside me, having been turned into a little mosquito by my story.

"Now you listen to me, see. If Trouble wants to tie up the final loose end, fifty thou's not going to cut it. It's going to be a hundred thousand, yeah, see, not fifty."

Vera smiled. Apparently my extortion pleased her. "The money's not a problem, Melvin. But you saved the worst for last. Smokey's not going to be as easy to get to. You're going to need a lot more than money to motivate you to get that bastard, see. You're going to need some real motivation."

"I don't understand why you didn't demand some

money," Elle said after a long period of silence as we walked toward Granmama's house. It was as if Elle had turned to cardboard after the meeting. The spring in her step was gone. She walked rigidly beside me, even reluctantly I'd say, because she tried to convince me that she was tired and it was getting cold and could she hop on a bus instead of accompanying me to Oriole Park; but I insisted. I was concerned about her. I didn't feel comfortable parting ways before I found out what was wrong. Also, I didn't find it all that implausible that we might end up on the beach after all. The standoff with Vera had built up my confidence.

"Vera was right," I said, puffing on my Russian. "I have no control. If she gives me money up front, I'll go off on a spending spree and will have no reason to finish the job. I'll probably fly off following Vaporee around the country like a groupie. I'd be cheating myself. It's a bigger score this way. Besides, I doubled my money, you should be happy."

"How do you know she'll even pay you?"

"I know her too well. If I go down, she goes down. She knows it."

"I don't think you know her that well," Elle whined, shaking her head like someone who got an F on an assignment she had stayed up all night working on.

"Oh dear Lord now what?" I blurted. I could see down the block that an ambulance and a police car were in front of Granmama's house. "Come on!" I demanded and started running. When I got to Granmama's I saw my sister Alice on the lawn wringing her hands. "What's going on?" I asked.

"Oh Mel," she cried and threw her arms over my shoulders, wetting my face with her sobs. "She was going door to door, trick or treating in the nude."

"She promised me she wouldn't do that." I was truly disappointed. I thought I had fixed it all with the Gold Plated YingYang.

"It's time, Mel. She can't be left alone any longer."

"That'll kill her," I sighed.

"I know. I know. But it has to be done. They're going to take her in for some tests. If she doesn't want to do it voluntarily," and her body thumped against mine as she sobbed, "we're going to have to force her."

"Listen," I said, shaking her. "We have to find a place; otherwise they'll throw her in some shit hole."

"I know. I know. They're so expensive though. We're going to have to sell the house. I know it. It happens all the time."

The front door opened and the paramedics came out wheeling Granmama strapped to a gurney. As they lifted her to get her down the front stoop, I could see her face, scared and confused. I approached and said, "Wait, that's my Granmama." I gently stroked her cheeks with my hands. "How are you doing?" I asked as if to a dying dog.

"Please, Mel, don't let them take me away."

"Shhhh. Calm down. They're just going to do some tests," I said, petting her ears. How pathetic my lie was. They had her strapped down like a mad person. "Here, this will calm you," and I put my Russian to her lips. She took a vape and her face brightened like a child taking a sip from a candy straw, and she blew out a cloud and laid her head down with a moan.

"What the hell are you doing?" one of the paramedics barked at me. "Get that away from her."

"It's okay, it's just vapor," I explained.

"Can't you see this woman is suffering from Alzheimer's," the other paramedic said in a hushed voice, although Granmama was right there and heard it and her eyes peered at him angrily. "Do you want to make it worse?"

I was about to give them a lecture about how safe vaping is but they huffed at me and rolled Granmama away toward the ambulance. "Don't worry Granmama," I called out. "I'll figure something out."

I don't know what's wrong with me sometimes, Yugo, but my mind gets so distracted. Even as they were lifting Granmama into the back of the ambulance, I started thinking about whether or not I should buy that Kanger Aerotank Turbo, trying to figure out what ohms two dual coils would come to, and which of my mechanical mods even had enough wattage to handle it, doing the math in my head even as Alice wrapped her arms around me again and cried. Granmama seemed secondary, a problem that just needed to be solved, and since the prospect of money was heading my way from two different directions, both from Vera and from my settlement, the 6 milliliter beast seemed more deserving of my stress. I had heard it produces a lot of vapor but not that much flavor and since it was sub-ohm I'd have to use a lower nicotine level juice with flavor shots, something I didn't have, so that would be an added expense.

Alice gave me the keys to the house and made me promise that I would double check that everything was okay before I locked it up, and I found Elle sitting on the stoop holding herself, shivering. "Come on, let's get inside and warm up," I said and she followed, looking deflated and trapped. "Give me a hand here," I asked as I started washing the dirty dishes in the sink with a scrub sponge and lemon scented Joy.

"What?" Elle asked, standing in the flickering fluorescent light on the dingy linoleum, near the doorway with a table separating us. She responded as if

I had asked her to jump off a cliff.

"Grab a towel," I suggested playfully. "You can dry."

"Look, Mel, I'm tired," she said without moving.

"Go in the parlor and lie down on the couch then," I instructed her.

Without hesitation she was off like a racehorse with the gate opening, complaining, "It smells like old lady in here," not in her usual playful way, but with a gag that I found insulting.

It took me about a half hour to clean up the kitchen and, wiping my soapy, wrinkled fingers on a towel, I came out and found Elle fast asleep on the couch, with one leg draped down to the floor and the other slung over the crest rail. I took off my trench coat and flung it onto the gondola chair and then spun my hat away with abandonment and I leapt on top of Elle, kissing her mouth passionately, the couch legs creaking under our weight. Her eyes popped open, bloodshot with tiny red lightning bolts, wider than I had ever seen them open before. I got my hand under her tube top, an atomizer falling out into the cushion crack, and I pulled the thin material up and wrapped my mouth around her breast like kissing the bottom of a soft and supple butternut squash. "Stop it," she said, struggling, but her movement below me only caused friction that aroused me. I pressed my bulge against her while my hand worked between the tight space between us attempting to unbutton her shorts. "I said stop it!" she screamed and I saw a bright white flash of light as something struck me across my temple and splattered across my face like a ball of sand. I fell off the couch and overturned a flimsy TV dinner tray. She had grabbed the salt sculpture of Granmama's dog Halo that was on the lamp table, and she had struck me with it so hard that it shattered into bits. I moaned, holding the side of my head.

Elle escaped over the armrest and stood near the front door. "What was that?" she yowled like a cat. "'What the hell was that?"

When I brought my hand off my head I saw it was dotted with blood. "Yugo. Please. Let me explain," I moaned as I crawled on the Afghan rug toward her. Yes, my dear, in my confusion I mistakenly called out your name, and I'm sure this is what really set Elle off.

She looked at herself, seeing that her tube top was still pulled up, and fixing herself, she howled, "Jesus Melvin! Jesus!!" and she stormed out of the house.

It wasn't her rejection of my advances that hurt the most, my dear, for when I came to the window and pulled away the lace curtain to look, I saw Elle untangle a carto tank that had managed to stay trapped in her clothing, and she threw it on the concrete, shattering it. She stood on the stoop, using one hand to yell into her cell phone in a small, angry voice, "I can't do this anymore! I'm finished!" while using her other hand to smoke a cigarette. Yes, my dear, a cigarette. I watched as she pocketed her phone, took a long draw and exhaled a cloud of smoke, and then she tossed the butt to the ground and extinguished it with her little canvas sneaker before dashing away under the yellow streetlamps. That was the last time I saw Elle.

Let me stop right here, my love. As you can see my tears are staining the pages, causing the ink to run. I will write back as soon as I regain my composure. Until then, know that besides vaping, you are all I think about.

XOXO,
Your Faithful Melvin.

Exhibit 33

Sketch discovered in pocket of highly dilapidated
trench coat discarded in Goodwill box
near Macy's on North Michigan Avenue.

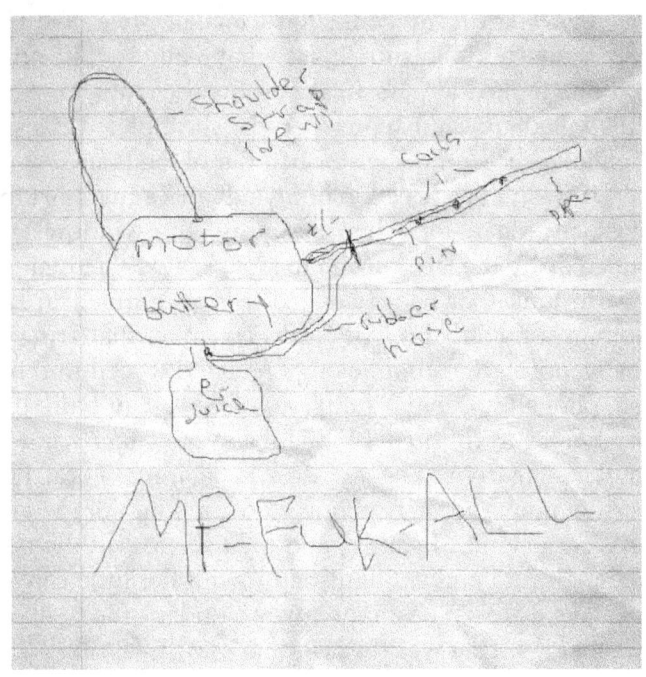

FINAL WRAP: Dry Burn

Dear Yugo,

I feel better today. I'm aware that I risk upsetting my lifted spirits by reliving the events of last autumn, but if I don't seize the opportunity now when I have an elevated mood, I may never be able to finish telling you what must be said. Just as it must have seemed to you that you woke in an alternative universe on that morning, when you found yourself adrift on a dinghy with your hair shaved off, so did it feel for me, as I watched Elle smoking a cigarette. She took a final drag, crushed the square under her foot and went away toward the street, disappearing behind the bushes. Moments later, Damian's Mitsubishi Lancer Evolution pulled into view and stopped. Its window came down and out came an arm that turned a blazing mounted spotlight on me, catching my face peering out in front of the curtains. As I jolted back out of view, Damian got out of his car and slammed the door. I grabbed my trench coat and trilby and rushed through Granmama's house, hurrying out the back door and across the back porch, and I tore through the yard, leaping over the wire mesh into the garden with an upsurge toward the shadowbox fence, when I was tackled around my waist like a bushel of twigs, my face smashing against the cheap, splintery wood. Down I went.

You are aware of the ways of the word, dear love, so I ask you: how am I responsible for what happened to Melany? She was drinking so many shots of Goldschlager at that party, I thought she would lay a golden egg when she staggered to the john. She was chain smoking her Viceroys and blowing the smoke out of a little opening at the side of her mouth like a radiator air valve. Was that not flirtatious? Couldn't it possibly be Damian's fault for abandoning her that evening? I was the one who got her home safely and let me tell you, it wasn't easy. Even though she lived a mere few blocks away, it literally took an hour of wandering around the neighborhood trying to figure out what she was slurring. Once we got there all she wanted to do was sleep on the musty smelling Oriental carpeting on the stairs of the apartment building. I was the one who had to wrap my hands under her armpits and drag her up, stair by stair. Imagine what might have happened if I *wasn't* there. I even had to go back downstairs and look at the mailboxes to figure out which apartment she lived in—not an easy task since I didn't even know her last name. I had to get her keys out of her jacket and fumble with them one by one until I figured it out. Sure, once I got her inside and dumped her on the bed, I could have left. But let's be honest. I didn't think that's what Melany *wanted*. After all, she was talking my ear off all evening, practically hanging all over me. Exactly why was I supposed to think she wanted anything less than what I did to her?

Having Damian pin me down in Granmama's garden reminded me of when my brother Porphy would sit on my chest after school, for hours at a time, only occasionally releasing his pressure so that I could catch a breath before I died. Granmama would walk into the house after work and Porphy would leap up and act like nothing was going on, even though I was blue faced on the floor struggling to breath. "You two behave yourselves," she would say, as if we were both equally responsible for my brother torturing me. She would plop her five pound string of keys onto the table and free herself of her sweater vest, sit on the gondola chair and kick off her shoes, falling asleep for the next hour like a charging battery.

Damian had me locked in place. "We can do this the easy way," he whispered into my ear as my face smeared into overripe tomatoes. "Or we can do it the hard way," and he twisted my arm painfully behind me.

After seeing Elle betray me with her cigarette, I had no fight left in me. "All right, all right," I groaned. "What do you want?"

I grimaced as he twisted my arm harder. His hot breath blew into my ear, "I want you to take a little ride with me. That's all."

"Okay, fine," I surrendered.

"I'm going to let you go now, and you're not going to try to make a run for it, are you," he told me, and I responded with the best affirmation that I could muster with my mouth pressed into the dirt. "If you try anything, it's really going to piss me off." I grunted that I understood so he abruptly let go of me, springing to his feet. My rising from the ground wasn't so nimble. I was swirling from both the physical and mental blow Elle had inflicted upon me, and it took time to catch my breath after having it squeezed out of me like a bagpipe. Damian stood in the garden in his Blackhawks windbreaker, out of which he produced a stogie. He patiently snipped the end of it with a fancy cutter and lit it with the lapping flame of a Dunhill, waiting for me as I kneeled and spit and panted. When I indicated that I was ready, Damian struck the cigar butt against the fence with a burst of sparks and helped me to my feet. I walked with him around the house to his car and when he opened the passenger side door for me, I threw myself in without resisting.

As he drove, I looked at the trees that were losing their colorful leaves and wondered where the year had gone. At that moment, I didn't care what Damian had planned for me; I cared about what I had been missing. I was so absorbed in my morbidity that I had neglected to notice the changing of the seasons. The prospect of winter scared me more than Damian did. They said another polar vortex was on its way; we know how that turned out.

"Do you mind if I have a vape?" I asked.

"You're kidding me, right?" Damian said without emotion. I didn't argue.

We arrived in front of a small brick cottage. Across the front of it, above the bay window, was strung a series of different colored letters cut from paper.

I T ' S A b O Y

It was clear the letters had been there for some time. The paper was curled and faded and the colors had bled with rain. The top of the B had come undone and flapped with the breeze, turning it from capital to lower case at the whim of the wind.

"Come on," Damian said as he got out of the car. I followed him through the door after he opened it with a key.

"Is everything okay," a voice I recognized as Melany's called out from above.

"Everything's fine," Damian called back.

He made the universal sign for me to be quiet as we came up the stairs and he placed his hand on my back, almost tenderly, and guided me through a doorway that he opened for me. I stood in the darkness for a moment before the light came on. In front of me was a crib, like an animal cage on legs made of wood.

"Go ahead," Damian coaxed as he stood behind me in the doorway, "have a look."

I took a step forward and looked at the mini Provario wrapped in a fluffy blanket with a polka dot infant cap on his peach sized head. Mini Provario looked up at me and smiled with a tooth as big as a grain of rice. A teardrop fell from my eye and splattered on his cheek, making his tiny eyelashes flutter. Damian handed me a handkerchief and I hid my face in it.

"Come on," he said, "let Damian, Jr. sleep." He flicked the light out and seeing that my knees were weak, he held me by the elbow and helped me down the stairs. He sat me down at his kitchen table and made us both a cup of instant coffee. We sat there for some time across from each other, taking sips, before he broke the silence. "What's wrong with you anyway?"

"Paranoid psychotic schizophrenia," I cried helplessly, "for starters."

It was as if the saliva Damian gasped in came out of his eyes as he struggled the way a man too macho to cry struggles. "No," he uttered through his face spasm. "I didn't mean that. I meant, why are you sobbing?"

I let it out like a fever breaking. "Because, I recognize him."

Damian slowly nodded his head with sad eyes like a settling bobblehead. For that brief instance we were two men sharing the inevitable cruelty of life, accepting the unavoidable hopelessness of it all, struggling not to blurt out like children, our lips trembling; but Damian soon enough gathered together a handful of napkins and blew his nose and wiped his face and inhaled deeply and said, "I just wanted you to know what you'll never have. I've accepted him. He's mine." There was an agonizing pain in my throat like I had swallowed a rock. "This is the one and only time I'm ever going to say this to you, Melvin. If you ever tell Melany, I'll kill you. As far as she's concerned, you got her home safely after the party and then you called *me* to come over; and when I arrived, you *left*. As far as she's concerned, before she woke, I was called off to work, and that's why she can't remember. Am I clear?" I stuck up a thumb, perhaps expressing too much relief. "I never want to see you again, you bastard. Ever."

I began to rise but Damian snapped, "Stay put!" casting me back down into my chair like a devil given a priestly command. He snatched the cordless phone from the counter and pressed an autodial button. "He's here," he said. "No, I mean right here. He's sitting in my kitchen. You're not going anywhere are you?" I shook my head earnestly. "He says he's not going anywhere. Okay." He leaned his butt against the dishwasher and said, "You can have a vape now."

I appreciated the gesture. I retrieved my Russian and took small puffs so that I didn't appear too obstinate. I got ten vapes from the opportunity before the doorbell rang. Damian disappeared and when he returned he was followed by two husky men, one of whom flipped open a leather badge holder for me, revealing a shiny gold eagle straddling the letters ATF. The other man was a sheriff's deputy. He threw a clump of folded papers onto the table. "Mr. Provario," he said, "you've been subpoenaed."

"Will you please come with us?" asked the ATF man. The question was rhetorical because as I stood I was immediately placed in handcuffs. They walked at my sides to a waiting Escalade.

Visions of Porphy pinning my wrists together as I lie on my chest in Granmama's yard came to mind. I've never figured out where Porphy came from. When we were growing up, he looked nothing like me or Alice. He was a particularly mean, bossy, blonde haired bully who never seemed happy unless he was causing someone pain or mental discomfort. To avoid him after school, I hid in the back aluminum shed, locking myself in by jamming a screwdriver into the mechanism. I would stay there for hours among the lawnmower and bags of mulch, until Granmama got home from work. It was peaceful in there, much better than having my face forced into piles of dog poop. Porphy would often remain outside the shed, creating a fake crying voice, saying, "Is the little girl hiding again? What's the matter little girl?" Sometimes it was a race between the two of us to see who could get home first. If I got home first I could make it to the shed and jam the lock with the screwdriver that I carried around with me for that very purpose; but if Porphy got home first, he would hide in the shed and upon my entrance, he would grab me and torture me for the next few hours. One summer day a big storm blew the shed over and it was discarded in the alley for the scrap collectors. So I found a new hiding place, the little room in the basement that once upon a time was used for storing coal. It took Porphy a while but eventually he wandered down, calling out, "Where's the little girl hiding?" After catching me, he made it a habit to dump dog poop into my hiding place whenever it was his turn to clean the yard. Eventually, I didn't come home at all. I hid under the porches of strangers, behind bushes, inside a garbage can, until one day I couldn't fit in the garbage can anymore.

It dawned upon me that I had grown as tall as Porphy. Out of the blue, I walked up to him and said, "I'm going to kick your ass," and I popped my fist against his cheek like a piece of raw fish hitting marble. It made a loud slapping sound but that was it. Psychologically, however, it mystified Porphy. He decided he would give me a good beating in return but his brute force was no longer affective against me. I laughed at him and slapped him back. We ended up wrestling, turning over furniture, knocking over lamps, even the Zenith was sent sliding across the room; and when Granmama came through the door I knew I had won. I was beat to crap, since Porphy was older, stronger and meaner after all, but Porphy had a scratch on his face that dribbled the tiniest bit of blood, and that was enough for me. I proved I could do damage.

"What in tarnation?" Granmama gasped, looking at the ransacked parlor.

I growled like a crazy person. "If you ever touch me again I'll stab you in your heart!" Porphy's mouth hung open. I could see it in his face. He believed me. The next time Porphy touched me was some twenty years later, when he was on leave and purposely greeted me with a vicelike shake that left me tending to my sore hand for half an hour. Once a prick; always a prick.

We were let through a gate at O'Hare Airport and it seemed we were driving on the runway for a while, before breaking away between two baggage convoys that flashed by both sides of the SUV. The doors opened and I was escorted to a hangar with a private airplane in it. A man in a windbreaker with a navy blue tie flying around came rushing up. I recognized him. It was Agent Maverick. I met Maverick that spring when I was apprehended after my room caught fire. He and Postal Inspector Doral and the old man from the Institute for the Preservation of the Institution of Cigarettes, whose name I never caught, had for all intents and purposes blackmailed me. They claimed they had me on a string of international trade violations concerning an online nicotine purchase, and they not so subtly let me know that to avoid prosecution I would have to do them the favor of testifying before the Joint Commission for Smoking Out E-Cig Myths. The hearing had been set up to get to the bottom of the ever growing, unregulated vaping industry. They believed my authority on the matter was that, as an individual, I had received more vape mail than anyone else, and those credentials would have to do in the absence of anyone willing to do their bidding for them. I was expected to say negative things about vaping to justify more e-cig legislation and regulations and outright bans. I learned soon enough that after a five week recess, the hearing would begin wrapping up in about fourteen hours. They may have caught me in the nick of time, but they couldn't have caught me at a worse time. The last thing I cared about at that moment was my freedom. In fact, spending some time in an isolated, closed place would seem like a gift. So sure, I'd stand before their committee, since they were forcing me to under threat of contempt anyway, but when I saw the old man from IPIC waving at me from the plane, with the collar of his shirt buttoned snugly against the wattles of his neck, showing his yellowed upper dentures with glee, I resolved then and there to say whatever the hell I pleased.

"Oh I don't think those restraints will be necessary," Agent Maverick called out. They unleashed me and surrendered me to him, and he wrapped his arm around me like I was his long lost pal, as I planted my palm against the top of my trilby to keep it from blowing away. He led me up a narrow, shaky set of rolling stairs to an opening in the plane that reminded me of a door to a wood oven.

As I entered the old man from the Institute greeted me. "Mr. Provario, glad to see you could make it," he said, cheerfully offering me his hand. It felt like raw duck. I was given a comfortable seat, offered a diet beverage and after a medical examination by a professional, I was allowed to vape. Honey, they really wanted to keep me happy. Two hours later we were landing at Ronald Reagan National Airport in Arlington. From there, I was whisked away by private car and then locked in a rather large, surprisingly expensive looking room at Le Méridien. It was like something out of the Jetsons.

I was scheduled to appear before the committee at 10 AM sharp, so they suggested I get some sleep. I was getting antsy since all my batteries were dead and I only had one charger with me that fit a mere 3.7 volt ego that didn't have pass through, so I plugged it in and had no choice but to wait until the battery was charged before I could use it. Instead of a bible in the bedside drawer, someone had left a copy of On the Road. Then I discovered the mini bar. I don't drink anymore, Yugo. Drinking and vaping don't mix; but I figured since I wasn't going to get a good bedtime vape, a nip or two wouldn't hurt. What a waste it was to get me a room at such a fancy hotel, because all I did all night was hide in the shower stall, unscrewing one tiny bottle of alcohol after another.

I didn't get any sleep at all. By the time Agent Maverick and the man from the Institute arrived at 8:30 AM in a vain attempt to prep me for my testimony, I was completely shit faced. They forced a few cups of coffee down my throat and before I knew it I was entering a large hall, surprised to see a decent audience in attendance. A group of e-cig activists, who had strung a banner off the balcony reading "This Hearing Brought to You by Big Tobacco", were being escorted out while I was being escorted in. In front of the hall was a raised platform, like a long pulpit designed for eleven different preachers, who sat smug and all powerful, each with their own microphone.

My name was called as if I was about to receive a

144

diploma and I stood in the aisle shouting back, "How can I help you?"

The institute man nudged me. "No, up there," and he pointed to a lone table with its own microphone. I stumbled over a loose shoestring and screeched the chair back and banged on the microphone to see if it was working, causing loud booms in the hall. "Test, test, one two three," I called out. The audience started laughing, so I took a bow for them and then for the television cameras. I had just taken a massive lung hit of some 36 mg citrus menthol and as I sat down it started having an argument with the alcohol in my veins. I could feel blood thumping in my skull and it was as if someone was flipping a gigantic, transparent deck of cards right in front of my face. I squinted, trying to focus my eyes to see the committee members. My sweet, I was about as plastered as Cynthia's cast of Hendrix's shlong, so don't hold me to any of this. If I'm mistaken about who was there, blame it on the two ounce bottles of Kahlua.

This is the way I remember it. Starting from the left I saw Jabba the Hutt who grew blond hair and whose face turned pink as she transformed into former New Mexico State Representative Liz Thompson. Next to her I saw Iggy Pop, but upon rubbing my eyes he morphed into the Governor of Michigan, Rick Snyder. I really got a scare when sitting next to him I saw Donald Rumsfeld but I soon realized it was just retiring Senator Tom Harkin from Iowa. I got a little thrill when I saw Annette Bening up there, but unfortunately when my eyes stopped blurring her name plaque read Barbara Boxer, Senator from California. Jack Reed, Senator from Rhode Island, sat next to her, pinching his nose closed with two of his fingers.

On the right side of the committee sat New Jersey

Governor Chris Christie eating a custard-filled long john. To the left of him was Connecticut Senator Chris Murphy with an odd, red faced, sweaty smile, like someone who had just been caught masturbating; and next to him was John Kasich, the Governor of Ohio, with one of those exaggerated frowns on his face, like someone caught in a sex scandal who was doing a photo op. I couldn't help but wonder what Murphy and Kasich were doing under their podiums. For a moment, I thought there was some hope when I saw Ron Paul sitting up there but unfortunately he morphed into Ed Markey, Senator from Massachusetts, and then I knew I was screwed. Next to him was a real Dick, Durbin that is, Senator from Illinois.

In the middle was the Mayor of Philadelphia, Michael Nutter, Chairman of the Committee; he banged a gavel and called for order when the crowd grew restless. "Hey, I know you!" I shouted at him. "Whazzup bro?" and I held up the black power fist. "By the way, where'd you get this chair, from the Salvation Army?"

"I'm sorry if the distinguished witness doesn't find the furniture to his liking," Rick Snyder stated facetiously.

"How long am I supposed to sit here?" I grumbled. "This chair'll give me hemorrhoids."

"Excuse me, will the witness please speak into the microphone," Mrs. Boxer requested.

I put my lips right up to it and said in a godlike voice that reverberated through the hall: "Hemorrhoids! Hemorrhoids!"

"Will the witness please take off his hat for the proceedings?" Liz piped in.

"Not on your life mister," I said to the delight of the audience.

"Please, we must insist," whined Mr. Kasich.

"You wanna come and try'n take it off me buster?" I asked.

Nutter banged his gavel to silence the commotion. "Let the man wear his hat if he wants to," he said. "He's obviously suffering from some sort of abnormality of the skull."

"I got your abnormality right here bud," I said.

"Order, order! Ladies and gentlemen, if you don't remain in order I'll have to ask you to leave. Now, will the witness please state his name for the record?"

"That would be Melvin Pro-to-the-v-to-the-a-to-the-r-to-i-to-the-o," and I tried to make some beat box noises but they just came out sloppy raspberries. From behind I could hear someone hissing. *Psssst! Psssst!* I looked back and saw the old man from the Institute waving at me and mouthing the words *What are you doing?* "Don't sweat it, Joe Camel. I got this," I slurred and blew him a kiss. Mr. Markey raised his hand and before Nutter could acknowledge him I called out, "The Senator from Massachusetts has the floor, woot!"

"I would like to ask the witness if he's ever received electronic cigarettes through the U.S. Mail," Markey said.

"Have I ever, Mr. Malarkey! I love me some vape mail. I'm addicted to vape mail. Waiting for the mailman makes me want to take a dump. I like to mix it up. Sometimes I get me some batteries, sometimes some cheap ass e-juice, sometimes a new atty or a tank, and sometimes just some wicks or wires or mesh or cotton balls. Every day is Christmas when you vape and the mailman is like a Santa Claus that just keeps on Clausing."

"Are you aware that sending cigarettes through the mail is illegal under the PACT Act?" he cautiously rebutted with a nod.

"Well, see, that's the thing. You're using the term electronic cigarette, but that's not very accurate. That's just what people call them for lack of a better word," I said as a rare moment of mental cohesion started developing. "The word cigarette suggests there's tobacco in them, but there isn't any. So I tell you what. Let's call them what they are, personal vaping devices, and we can all pack up and go home."

The committee fidgeted and mumbled to themselves, all of them except for Christie, who was now working on a big frosting covered bear claw.

"But, isn't it true that the liquid used in these personal vaping devices contains the same chemicals used in antifreeze?" Mr. Durbin asked slyly.

"Hey, Dick, you know what else is in antifreeze? Water! Is water bad for you? Must be, it's in antifreeze, ain't it? Come off it, Dick. You know, they've invented this really nifty thing. It's called the internet. Learn to use it. The so-called antifreeze used to make e-juice is the same stuff they put in gel caps and salad dressings. Are you going to have a joint commission on the safety of salad dressing next? Why not? It contains the same ingredients!"

"I object to that comparison," shouted Tom Harkin, who was quite agitated. "So called e-cigarettes contain nicotine and it's proven that nicotine causes cancer!"

"No it has not!" I shouted back, my arm flailing. Behind me I could hear the man from the Institute spitting *Melvin! Melvin! Remember our deal!* "The only studies of nicotine have concerned nicotine *in smoke*. Smoke. Got it? There isn't any smoke in vapor. There's been no study of the effects of nicotine in vapor."

"Oh, I doubt that very much," Harkin argued.

"Then produce it," I shouted. "I'm sure you

prepared yourself for this hearing, Senator. Surely if you're going to make such a baseless accusation, you must have before you a copy of some study to prove it."

"Well, I don't have it right here before me, but I'm sure—"

"Shut up then!" I raved and the crowd began cheering hysterically, causing Nutter to whack his gavel so hard I expected to see sparks.

"But how do you know it's safe?" Chris Murphy interrupted inquisitively. "What if it's not? Aren't you gambling with your health?"

"First off, I'd like to remind this committee and everyone here today and everyone at home in TV land, this is MY body! What I put in my own body is my business. Do I look like I'm five years old to you? Don't you think I can decide for myself what's safe for me? I look at the ingredients in e-juice and it's all FDA approved for consumption. So in what whacko world does combining FDA approved ingredients result in something poisonous? Suuuuure, maybe there are *some* risks. It's early in the game. Products are still being developed and improved. Maybe I'm inhaling some minute amounts of heavy metals or maybe some things in the flavorings aren't that good for me. But you know what I'm not inhaling? Smoke! And smoke has been proven, I repeat, proven to cause cancer, as well as a hundred other diseases. So the question isn't how do I know if it's safe," and I turned and raised my arms, addressing the audience. "The question is how do these yokels know that it's *not* safe!" My ears rattled with the applause.

The man from the Institute withered and slunk down into a chair at the back of the room.

I heard a voice say, "But aren't jeesh jings marketish ta chiljin?"

I turned to Chris Christie and said, "What the flood did you say?"

"Shorry," he said and poured himself a cup of water and swallowed his mouthful of fritter. "I was saying," he continued, wiping the side of his mouth with the back of his hand, "some of these e-juices are flavored like candy and deserts. Doesn't that mean they're being marketed to children?"

"Gee, I don't know, Chris. Is that bun you're chomping on being marketed to children? It tastes good doesn't it? Do kids have a monopoly on stuff that tastes good? Why do you want my vape to taste like shit?"

"Will the witness please watch his language," Nutter shouted.

"Listen, all of you," I declared. "No reputable vape vendor that I know of is trying to sell to kids. They don't have to. It's a billion dollar industry as it is. There's no shortage of an adult market. You just don't have faith in people's morality and that's what's sad. You think just because it tastes like a gummy bear people are going to sell it to six year olds? That's ridiculous. If any one of you can produce one single study proving that children have been purchasing e-cigs first hand, instead of getting them some other way, the same way they would get cigarettes anyway, if any of you can produce a study proving that proportionally more children have been starting to vape than otherwise would start to smoke, then provide it, otherwise all we're doing here is debating your paranoid delusions and your pessimistic worst case scenarios. I know I don't give my e-cigs to kids. Do any of you give your e-cigs to kids?" I shouted at the audience. Several people shouted out *No* and *No way* and *Hell no*. "All you guys sitting up there, you stuffed shirts with nothing better to do, you're so wrapped up

150

in your desire to control everything that you're missing the big picture. There are millions of vapers today and tomorrow there will be millions more. That's millions of people who aren't smoking cigarettes, millions of people who won't get lung cancer, who won't drain the tax payers when they get sick without insurance. Millions of people who aren't polluting the environment with second hand smoke. And you want to do what about it, ban it? Why? What kind of twisted, illogical reasoning is that? Is Big Tobacco contributing to your campaign funds or what?" The audience was really getting riled up. It felt like I was leading a lynch mob. Nutter banged for order.

"Seriously, what are we even doing here? Why aren't you out trying to catch a serial rapist or a mass murderer? I bet you spent more money on this e-cig witch hunt than you did investigating nine-eleven. But let me tell you, you and you and you and you and you, you can't stop it. It's too late. It's already grown too big. You can't rip out a chunk of the economy as large as the vaping industry without repercussions. What do you want to do? Put thousands of people out of work, rob the struggling post office of millions of dollars in revenue, take billions of dollars of commerce out of the hands of respectable small businesses and hand it right back to Big Tobacco? Is that what you're proposing? Well let's see how well that fares you at the polls, and I'm talking to *you* Liz. I say, no way! Smoking is dead. Vaping is the future!" I twirled around and shouted it again. "Smoking is dead. Vaping is the future!" The crowd began to chant with me as I pumped my fists: "Smoking is dead. Vaping is the future!" Louder and louder. "Smoking is dead. Vaping is the future!" Bang, bang, bang, bang, bang, bang, bang.

As the crowd settled down I could see the old man

from the Institute exiting the room, the door closing harshly behind him with a rush of air.

"If the committee wouldn't mind," Jack Reed said. "I was wondering if the witness could give us a little demonstration on how he uses an electronic cigarette."

"If the committee has no objections," Nutter said, "I think we can allow it."

"Now? Right here?" I asked.

"Yes, please, if you would be so kind. Do you have one of those personal vaping devices on you?" Mr. Reed asked.

"Oh hells yeah, I have all sorts of shit," I said, tapping my various trench coat pockets. "And I have a freshly charged ego too. Let's see." I started pulling items out of my pockets and plopped them onto the table. A television camera came rolling up toward me, zooming in on my hands as I arranged my items. I gave C-SPAN a step by step explanation as I used a 1.4 millimeter screwdriver to wrap dual three ohm coils made of pre-oxidized kanthal through the posts of an atomizer. Through the coil I inserted a twisted string of cotton, doused it with juice, assembled the gadget and I was ready to vape. "Did anyone time that?" I called out. Someone in the audience shouted out, *About three and a half minutes.* "I guess that means I'm no longer a newbie.

"You see, vaping is nothing like smoking," I explained. "You have to pull the vapor in slowly, like this," and I took a vape, "and you don't even need to inhale to absorb the nicotine," I said through the exiting vapor. "Vapor is composed of water molecules, which are ten times larger than smoke molecules, so the nicotine will absorb more efficiently through your mouth and nasal cavity than it will in your lungs. To produce more vapor, it helps to perform what famous vape critic Bill Picardo, who I see in the audience today—that's right, I'm vape dropping, waddup Bill—what Bill calls slip streaming. That is, sucking in some air from the side of your mouth while you vape like this," and I demonstrated and blew out a huge cloud. "Of course there's nothing wrong with lung hitting. I do it all the time.

"Actually, let me demonstrate some of my personal vaping techniques. This is called the Fruit Loop," and I sucked in some vapor and held it in my mouth as I puckered my lips and then I poked my cheek with my finger rapidly, producing several tiny vape rings that floated in front of my face. In response I was met with silence. A bead of sweat formed on my brow. "Okay, then. This is called the Double French Kiss," I said, taking in a vape and wiggling my tongue around as the vapor exited my mouth, was sucked up into my nose, came out of my mouth again and was sucked up by my nostrils yet again. I expected the committee to hold up score cards but instead I received mediocre applause from the audience. "Hmm. Tough crowd, eh?" I uttered. "This is what I call the Ring Around the Rosy," and I took a big mouth hit off the atty, blew out a thick ball of vapor and then quickly followed that with a vape ring that travelled faster and surrounded the ball as it expanded into the shape of a rose. The applause was a little more enthusiastic but the committee members sat staring at me. "Okay, how about the Disappearing Ghost?" I challenged, taking the biggest vape I could muster. I slowly let out a massive, thick as cream cloud, and then I sucked the entire thing out of the air, right back into my mouth, not leaving a trace. I held my breath until I became dizzy and when I exhaled, it was invisible. That one got a pretty good response from the crowd but the committee remained as unmoved as mannequins. "Well, okay, then. Let me bring out the big guns! Now I will perform what I like to call the Sloppy Drunk Ass Anovape," I announced.

I got my belt unbuckled, but Nutter banged his gavel and declared, "This witness is excused," and a team of uniformed guards surrounded me and escorted me out of the hall as my slacks started falling down. I was dumped out of the hearing room like a midget to a dartboard, where Agent Maverick and the man from the Institute were waiting for me as I pulled up my drawers. I apathetically put my hands out, wrist to wrist, so they could be cuffed.

"You don't know who you just screwed with, Provario," the Institute man said.

"So you're going to leave me hanging?" I asked Agent Maverick as I attempted to surrender. Maverick looked embarrassed as he shook his head and smiled. My arms dropped to my sides. "So it was all a ruse," I said. "You never had anything on me. All that stuff about the nicotine from the Middle East. It was a smoke screen. It was a bluff to get me here today, to do your bidding."

"You have no idea the reach IPIC has," the old man gurgled as Agent Maverick walked away, his head sinking.

"It's not I-Pick!" I blasted. "It's I-Piss! The C in Cigarette is soft!"

"You haven't seen the last of me, Melvin Provario," he swore as he followed Maverick down the hall.

"Tell it to me lawyers!" I said.

I slept my hangover off on a wood bench that reminded me of a Catholic church and I came to as the committee hearing was being let out. There was Bill Picardo, internet vaping critic, in the chattering crowd. I followed him outside to a food truck and called out his name. He turned and upon seeing me, he shouted, "You!" and for a second I thought I was busted for stealing his Gold Plated YingYang, but then he laughed and said, "You're my new hero."

I rushed up to him. "Let me use your phone," I begged, and Bill kindly did, continuing to comment on the display I had made as he chomped on a hot dog. I wasn't listening to him. I was calling my sister Alice for an update on Granmama.

"She's doing better," she said. "She's still in the hospital but we have to find her a place soon, Mel. Who knows what will happen next time?" I was nodding, saying, "Yes, yes, I know," to Alice and to Bill at the same time. "Listen, Mel, I've been looking online and I think I've found the perfect place for her. It's called Saint Sebastian's and it's in Kissimmee, Florida."

"Oh, Granmama will never go for Florida."

"No wait, just listen to this," and I could hear her rustling some papers. "Saint Sebastian's Assisted Living is a place where seasoned adults can truly let it all shine. Our vintage residents bask in the sun of our sandy beach and relax in the shade of our magnificent oak trees. Your loved ones will find it easy to put aside their worries as our professionally trained staff does all the work for them. Our golden residents enjoy shuffleboard, cribbage tournaments, fishing trips, outdoor movie nights and many other nightly events. Saint Sebastian's has all the amenities that a clothes free retirement facility should have."

"Wait, did you say clothes free?"

She kept on reading. "And, since we're located in the heart of Central Florida, you will find yourself minutes from area attractions when you come to visit your loved ones."

"So it's a nudist colony for old folks?" I asked and

Bill Picardo gave me a little look.

"More like a nudist condo complex for retired people, about a half hour from Disney World," she confirmed.

"Sounds expensive," I said.

"Yeah, well, that's the thing," she said losing steam. "We'd definitely have to sell the house. And then we'd still need about fifty grand."

"Listen, sis, I think you're on to something. How much time do we have?"

"They have an opening now," she urged.

"Ok, we're going to talk again. Don't lose hope," and I hung up and spoke like a pathetic begging child, "Can I make another call?" Bill nodded. I called directory assistance and got put through to UIC's Institute for Health Research and Policy and asked to be connected to the office of Professor Chas Fraloupka. A girl answered. "Is Elle there?" I asked. *Who?* "Elle, the intern." *I'm the intern, sir.* "Look, I know she probably doesn't want to talk to me, but if she's there could you please—"

"Sir, I'm telling you. I've been the intern for nearly a year. There's no one named Elle here." I quickly decided to forgive Elle for lying to me about her job. I decided not to even mention it to her when we were reunited.

I tossed the phone to Bill and then gave him a fist bump. "By the way, I loved your review of Stratagem."

"Funny you should mention that," he said. "I recorded that review when I was at the Vaporee Festival, and the crappiest thing happened in my hotel room—"

I spotted Mike Crow with his camera around his neck in the distance. "I'm sure it's a hellava story, Bill," I said, giving him a pat on his back, "but I gotta split." I started to run after Mike but I stopped to turn around and I made a thundery sound and I hollered, "Taste the Juice!!" Bill smiled and waved at me. When I caught up to Mike I nearly knocked him off his feet as I grabbed his shoulder and spun him around. "Mike, Mike, you gotta help me. I'm stranded. Please tell me you're heading back to Chicago."

Mike stepped back and looked at me in contemplation. "Okay, Melvin, you can hitch a ride with me, under one condition."

"What's that?"

His condition was that he wanted video footage of me getting kicked out of the Lincoln Memorial for vaping, which would be valuable to his website after my testimony aired on C-SPAN. So I obliged and it was nothing but a thing. I stood before the great statue of Lincoln sitting in his chair, pulled out my newly built atty and had a vape and within seconds I was surrounded by Homeland Security and asked to leave the premises. I looked over to Mike who was taping, and he made a gesture suggesting I should play along a little longer, so I defiantly had another vape and was forcefully ejected, literally by the seat of my pants.

"Priceless," Mike Crow said.

I expected Mike to have a Volkswagen minibus that ran off of compost, but he had rented a Hummer. He jumped inside and it took thirty seconds for him to reach over to the passenger's side door to open it and he reached down to help me up. I felt safe. No DC sniper would get a shot at me in that thing. We shared a tank of Pelican by Caterpillar, using our own drip tips, during our long journey back to Chicago.

Did you know that I hold a Bachelor's degree in Elementary Education? After receiving my teaching certificate and going through an internship program, I was given my own kindergarten class at the Riverside Children's Academy. It was during my third year that my class was disproportionately composed of strikingly beautiful little girls, whose names I still recall but should not be uttered. Out of nineteen kids, thirteen of them were female, the offspring of some of the wealthiest and most handsome families in Chicago. The variety of their charm was overwhelming. Each day I stood before a mesmerizing sea of bright blue or subtle brown eyes and long braided or wild, curly hair from children who seemed to have the intelligence of at least second graders and who dressed like fashion queens. I was convinced they were our future super models and movie actresses and it was intimidating. To try me further, this gang of nymphs insisted on making physical contact with me every chance they got, holding my hand, volunteering to sit on my lap during story time, crawling all over me during playtime.

For a while, I struggled with what I was feeling, but over time I convinced myself that there is nothing wrong with recognizing and enjoying beauty, so instead of fighting my impulses, I embraced them. I rearranged the seating order, placing the girls I found to be the most gorgeous in the front, positioning the miniature desks zigzaggedly so there was never a face hidden from me. I put all the boys together in the back. My private affection was innocuous at first, but I admit I started taking it to another level.

One day I brought a Polaroid to class and took snapshots of each of my girls and arranged them on the shelves of a big hutch in my Hyde Park apartment. Every day one of my ladies was assigned a show and tell task that required she bring in something personal; it had to come from her bedroom, something uniquely hers. The items ranged from erasers to dolls to ribbons to crayons and even one little sock. I bagged the items with the owner's name on them and put them in a box that I took home with me every night, promising at the end of the year everyone would get their stuff back. As I rubbed my hands against their possessions on the hutch that had turned into a shrine, I was fully aware that having a crush on thirteen preschoolers was absurd, but I figured, as long as I kept it innocent, it was harmless, so why fight it when it felt so good?

I taught my tiny girlfriends a game that we'd perform at the drop of a hat. One of them would stand in front of the class as I stood behind it, and I would recite out riddles that I had created. "What do you skin when you climb a tree?" I would call out and the class would shout in unison, *You're knee!* and the little girl at the front would lift her dress and show us what a five year old Native America knee looks like. "What do you twist when you're not too careful?" *Your ankle!* And she would pull down her sock to show us her Chinese flesh. "What keeps your arm attached to your body?" *Your shoulder!* And she would unbutton the top of her blouse and pull it aside to show us what Norwegian freckles look like. "What will get big if you eat like a glutton?" *Your belly button!* That one caused hysterics as my little chocolate bar lifted up her sweater to show her Peruvian navel. From time to time a class monitor would enter the room unexpectedly and when that happened, I recited only certain riddles with answers like: *Your nose! Your ear! Your hair!* Otherwise, I took lots of Polaroids, promising a scrapbook at the end of the year.

During nap time I would slide a file cabinet slightly over the edge of the door as an alarm if a monitor entered, as I lie on one of the mats, inches from a sleeping child, propped up on one arm so that I could admire a pretty face at a proximity and for a duration not offered to me otherwise.

We also played a game that was quite risky considering I would have no excuse if a monitor decided to pop in. The room had a small closet for toys. I had cleared enough of it to fit in a chair. I would sit on that chair in the closet with the door closed, with a child on my lap. The game was that we were a prince and a princess, held prisoner in a castle by an evil king, who could only be defeated by the alphabet. Only after the class recited the entire thing would we be set free. Some of the children were afraid of the dark, so I held them tight and whispered soothing things in their ears, as the class outside slowly sang out their monotonous letters. When they got to Z the closet door would fly open and out I would come, spinning around with my little princess lifted above my head, giving the class a thrill. I may have had my strange ways, my dear Yugo, but I was a good teacher. How many kindergartners do you know who can recite their ABCs? Many of my students went on to become geniuses and I'm sure it was because I set them on the right path early on in life.

One night I had a horrible nightmare. In it, I had all my little dandelions spit into a Styrofoam cup for me, until it was half filled with saliva. I sealed it with a lid and put it in my lunchbox and brought it home with me. In the dream, I had a major argument with myself and boy was it a doozy. My attempts to fight the urge were in vain however, because that ugly half of me was determined and persuasive. I was alone, he insisted. Nobody would know. I took the cup of spit to bed with me and poured it into the palm of my hand and like magic the mouths of all thirteen of my ladies appeared, like open blisters, across my thumb and finger as I made a fist.

I awoke rolling around, drenched with sweat. Everything had changed. It no longer felt innocent. I was concerned for my girls, concerned that I had become a threat to them. I'm not a religious man, Yugo, but that morning I prayed. To what, exactly, I don't know; but I prayed, prayed for the safety of my little girls, and the answer to my prayer was swift. My appeal was interrupted by a phone call asking me not to come to work, that I should instead report to the office the next day before hours. In my absence, my young loves were interviewed by a child psychologist who decided I should never see them again. I gathered up the Polaroids and the children's possessions and put them in a box that I wrapped in a bag that I put in a bigger box that I tied up in an even bigger bag, and I carried it through the alleys, taking it blocks away to throw it into a random dumpster. That was a wise move, because the next day, when I was in the office being informed of my dismissal, the police handed a search warrant to my landlord who opened my door for them and allowed them to inspect. I gained some small relief when I learned it wasn't one of my darlings who had betrayed me, but one of the boys, who was jealous because I never allowed him to participate in the games. He complained to his parents, who were shocked to learn about the Polaroids.

I wasn't arrested and there was never anything about me in any newspaper, but I became paranoid nonetheless, convinced everyone around me knew about my nightmare. I began hiding my face under a wide brimmed hat and I covered my body with a long coat, so that I wouldn't be recognized. My dear Yugo, you are the second person that I've told this story to. The first person was Mike Crow, on our way back to Chicago in the Hummer he had rented. Upon being let out in Bridgeport on that terribly windy Halloween morning, I reminded him that the stories I shared with him on the road were off the record, and he agreed, nodding his pale, weary face and not uttering a sound.

As I battled the frigid wind back to my cubbyhole on Canalport, I passed the Balance Vape Den, or I should say what used to be the vape den, as it was already cleared out with a bright orange for rent sign in the window. I snickered. How did they expect to stay open with nothing but the same two dweebs for customers? Seeing that uppity vape den closed may have lifted my spirits, but what I found next made me do a jig.

I was rummaging through the Bieberman mail as usual when I discovered an envelope with a window on it addressed to me. Behind the window was green paper that certainly looked like a check, but it was too early for my disability to arrive. When I looked at the return address my stomach nearly swallowed up my chest. *Goldstein, Silverberg and Pearlman.* I carried it to the back porch, gripping it so it wouldn't blow away as I tried to peel the glued flap off, and when I was halfway up the stairs I lost patience and ripped it open and pulled out the check. It probably took exactly one second for me to go from disappointment when I saw the number 185 ($185 dollars? Is that all?) to crapping my pants when I saw the comma followed by three zeros. I had to sit down, right there on the porch floor near the ladder to the attic. I must have looked at that check for ten minutes, just to make sure I wasn't hallucinating, before I burst out in laughter and jumped up to perform a scene from Riverdance. I climbed up the ladder and pulled myself in to say farewell to the room with the hole in the roof sealed by the blue tarp that was snapping in the wind, when I heard the cell phone that was charging on my work table playing Smoke on the Water. I answered it and after a brief period of silence, Elle spoke. "Mel?"

"Elle, is that you?"

"I hope you don't mind. I purchased some minutes for you."

"That's sweet!" I said joyfully. "Listen, about what happened—"

"That was my fault, Mel," she said to my delight. "I don't know why I reacted like that. Did I hurt you?"

"Naw. There was actually a doctor on the plane. He gave me a stitch."

"You were on a plane?" she asked, bewildered.

"It's a long story, Elle. You won't believe it."

"Mel, do you still want to be with me?" she asked.

"Yes, yes!" I anxiously insisted. "Yes of course I do!"

"Maybe with Vera's money, we could go away together. Be together."

"Elle, listen to me. You're not going to believe it. I got my settlement check. It's way more than what I was expecting. I mean waaaay more," I laughed. "I don't have to do what Vera wants anymore. We can take off right now, anywhere you want to."

"What, wait, but you got it?" Elle stuttered, like someone trying to improvise after receiving a botched line. "But, what about Vera?"

"Honey, I'm telling you, I'm loaded. Forget that bitch," I assured her.

"Hold on," she said and I held on for a few moments until she was back. "That's great news, Mel. But we can't leave Vera hanging. You have to let her know."

"Oh forget that cow," I said. "Who cares about her?"

"I'm serious, Mel," she said sternly. "It wouldn't be right. She'll be wondering where you are. You have to let her know. Plus she owes you money. Doesn't she?"

"What do you suggest?" I asked, persuaded by her urgency.

"Why don't we meet her together? Tonight. We'll tell her together, that you're done with her. She'll just have to find someone else to finish it. That'll put an end to it once and for all. Together, Skippy, you and me." She sounded as if she was crying.

"Okay," I said.

"I'll meet you at her motel room at eight tonight," she concluded with a sniffle.

"Eight tonight," I repeated.

"You'll be there, won't you?" she begged.

"I'll be there, I promise," I assured her.

"I love you Mel," she said and we were disconnected.

My mind see-sawed back and forth between the glory of hearing Elle confess her love to me and something else that gnawed at me: since when did Elle know about Vera's motel room? But why second guess good fortune. Right? I was suddenly wealthy and it was only a matter of hours before I would no longer be alone. Vera would be off my back too. That alone would be tantamount to having a pus filled boil lanced.

I couldn't exactly go to a Currency Exchange and cash my check, and depositing it into a bank would expose it to all sorts of risks that I don't want to bore you with, so I kept it in the inside breast pocket of my trench coat until I could think my strategy through. I gathered together whatever loose change I had and bought Elle a bouquet of flowers. It got damaged in the wind so I placed a bottle of Vanilla Cupcake from The Vapor Room inside of it, one of Elle's favorites, and I didn't want to put my new future in the hands of the CTA, so that evening I tempted fate by using the Toyota Camry. It had stolen plates and bullet damage across the windshield but I found it right where I had left it, parked in the rickety garage of an abandoned house otherwise unmolested.

Oh the plans I concocted on my way to the motel that chilly Halloween evening. In my mind Elle and I were already under a bear skin rug in a pleasantly damp, cool cave on some exotic island. On the walls there was caveman art and just outside there was a glorious waterfall splashing into a sparkling blue lagoon that we would swim in after making love. Elle looked up at me through her seductive slits as I penetrated her for the first time and her face twisted with pain and she said it to me again. "I love you." And as I reached my climax she begged for me not to pull out, for we would have a child and this one I would keep and love and protect. Eventually I told her about you, Yugo; and she was cool with it. We tracked you down and invited you into our family. I had both of you as my lovers, and the two of you became lovers, and the three of us were lovers; and the two of you dressed up like school girls and all our wildest fantasies came true. I got out of the Camry with the battered bouquet as sparse snowflakes began falling, and I jogged up the motel stairs still throbbing from my fancy. When I knocked on Vera's door, it creaked open.

I stepped inside to announce myself and all my dreams shattered. Vera was sprawled out on the bed, her blood soaked face hanging limply off the mattress, with a deep gash in her throat. Slowly I looked up to see blood, smeared by someone's fingers into the shape of the Ziggy logo, still dripping on the wall above the headboard. And to my horror, I turned to see what could only be described as a severed head with snow white hair in a puddle of blood on the floor.

"Elle!" I cried out.

One moment I was standing in Vera's motel room, and the next moment Mr. Vape was sitting in the Camry, half a block down from Smokey's Tavern, with the MP-FUK-ALL on his lap. He put the car in drive, slammed his foot on the gas and kept it there as he accelerated down the street. Mr. Vape then pulled the steering wheel sharply to the left and the tires screamed as the car made a ninety degree skidding turn, the bouncer slamming face first into the windshield like a smashed pumpkin as the Camry crashed through the front door of the tavern, taking part of the wall down with it; the car continued through and crashed into a pool table before coming to a halt.

Mr. Vape came out wielding the FUK-ALL, shooting a stream of flaming bubblegum flavored napalm from it. The first one he shot at was the bartender, who was in the panicky process of pumping a shotgun that unloaded into the tray of beers the topless waitress was carrying when Mr. Vape roared, "Vape on this!" and gave him a splash to the face. Next he spun around and sprayed as many torsos as he could as the place erupted into a firework display of gunfire. Bullets ricocheted off the car door as he used it for cover, sending long, fiery streaks through the open window. The wind gushed in swirling the fire around.

The door to the meeting room opened and Phil Zigfield stood there in the smoke, his teeth parted and his eyes jittering with horror. His tavern had literally turned into a scene from a deep part of Hades. People were screaming and wriggling about as they escaped. When Mr. Vape saw someone escaping who wasn't yet on fire, he aimed and gave him a glowing blast of sizzling retribution.

Smokey called out, "What the hell?" and tumbled back into the meeting room. Mr. Vape gave chase through the flames, the bottom of his trench coat catching fire. As he dashed into the room, Smokey's arms were recklessly smashing through the glass of a gun case on the wall. His bloody hands fumbled with a Tommy gun as Mr. Vape leapt onto the thick table and charged toward him. As Smokey turned with a curse to aim, the pipe of the FUK-ALL went into his mouth.

"Smoking is dead," Mr. Vape said and he flipped the switch. Flames shot out of Smokey's nose like two mini blow torches. The Tommy gun flashed at his side, ripping holes into the wall as if it was made out of paper, spent shells popping out and bouncing on the table at Mr. Vape's feet like so many gold teeth. Mr. Vape looked into Smokey's boiling eyes. "How's that for throat hit?" he asked. Swirls of smoke came out of Smokey's ears. When Mr. Vape released the FUK-ALL, Smokey collapsed into the broken glass and slid to the floor, his face blistered and steaming, the Tommy gun continuing to rip the ceiling to shreds until it was out of bullets.

Mr. Vape made his escape, sliding the false wall away only to find the back door locked. He attempted a break for it through the bar, but the wind had turned it into a furnace and the blazing heat pushed him back as he shielded his face with his arm. He was trapped. The smoke was choking him and at the rate the fire was spreading, he would be engulfed in no time. So he resolved that he would at least die with the satisfaction of knowing that he avenged Elle's death and that he had stomped out the last of the Ziggies. It seemed a dignified death to him, a proper end to his story. As the stacks of cardboard boxes in the room caught fire, he tried to tidy himself, attempted to wipe the burn holes off his coat. He adjusted the scorched brim of his trilby with pride and as the walls around him combusted, he pulled out his Russian to have what he expected to be the final vape of his life, when the door opened and an arm came through and grabbed him by the coat and yanked him out into the alley. He went face first onto the pavement and before he could rise he heard a car door slam and watched tail lights speed away. The wind had blown the cardboard away and there was Brandon's bike, still hidden behind the dumpster. He mounted it as the approaching sirens wailed and thus began his long, grueling, all night battle against a lake effect snowstorm to get home.

I slept for two days and then hid in the attic for a few more, crapping in a bucket so that I wouldn't have to show my face to anyone. After about a week, I came out, unshaven and shielding my eyes from the sunlight. I don't watch TV, Yugo. That's probably why I've never been brainwashed. But after I came out of the attic, feeling as if I had been born into a new world, my wealth still in my breast pocket, the possibilities still not fully considered, I found myself in the Micro Center looking to see if they carried Nichrome; that's when I wandered into their television room. There were at least twenty screens on the walls all playing the same news. Larry's car was being dragged out of the river by a truck with a mechanical cable. Firemen were shooting water into the gutted out tavern. Photos of the five Zigfields were showed. But the correspondent was reporting that Phil Zigfield and four of his *sons* had all been murdered in separate incidents, leaving investigators baffled and with very few clues.

Surely they had it wrong. I felt like calling the station to correct them. I approached one of the televisions and changed the channel. The next news program was reporting it the same way. How could Vera not know Smokey was their father? How did Elle know about Vera's motel room? Why would Sandra recommend me to a perfect stranger anyway? How did Vera know so much about the Zigfields? How did Phil learn about Vera? And if Phil killed Vera and Elle, then why was he just hanging around his hideout an hour later as if nothing had happened?

"Stop beating yourself up," Mr. Vape suggested. "The only question you should be asking is what you're going to do with your money." I laughed, drawing attention to myself. "I could buy every one of these TVs if I wanted to," I shouted at them.

I decided. I would open a bank account and as soon as the check cleared, I would start making large withdraws. I would rent safety deposit boxes in ten other banks, and keep my cash spread out like that. I headed to the Bieberman house to get the identification that I would need to do this. Finally I was feeling good. A lot of bad things happened, but I had a fat check and that day promised to be the first day of the rest of my life. I climbed up the aluminum ladder and pulled myself into the attic and reached up and pulled the chain. The light bulb came on and I saw a familiar face, sitting on the chair in the middle of the room, in precisely the same spot Vera sat when I first met her. It was the Inside Man. There was a bulging backpack on the plywood next to him. His hand was resting on his lap, holding a thick revolver that was casually pointing at me.

"Pull up a chair, Melvin," he said. I kept my eye on him as I ducked to avoid the nails, taking the kitchen chair away from my work table and setting it in front of him. I hadn't killed all the Ziggies after all. The Inside

Man had the same logo tattooed on his hand between his thumb and pointer.

"I saw on the news," I muttered as I sat, "that Phil wasn't their brother."

He nodded. "Phil was my father," he confirmed. "I'm the fifth brother. The adopted one."

"May I ask your name?"

He laughed. "My name is—" and he began rapidly stuttering out syllables. "Mamanana-rarasasa-tatavava. Vava? Veve?"

"Vera!"

He spoke in Vera's hoarse voice. "I was actually going to say Victor."

"That was *you*, all along? You made yourself up like a woman? Why?"

"Why not? Would you have sympathized with *this* mug?"

"But what about Patty?"

"Who's Patty?" he asked, shrugging.

"You said your father passed away," I reminded him.

"He did. You killed him," he said.

"But the inheritance."

"You mean the multimillion dollar cancer stick ring?" he corrected. "Smoking is so passé. I've been trying to quit, but they just wouldn't let me."

"But I saw you. I mean Vera. Or was it you? I saw you in the motel room, with your throat cut."

"Makeup," he said, shrugging one shoulder.

"And Elle?" I shouted. "What about Elle?"

"A Halloween mask," he said. "I'm surprised you fell for it. I can't imagine what I would have done if you wanted to touch it."

"So where's Elle?" I pressed, seeing a glimmer of hope.

"She's safe."

"Where is she? I want to see her."

Victor Zigfield lifted his gun from his lap. "Are you still deluding yourself? There is no Elle. There never was. She's a good little thief who works for me, nothing more. Why would a young girl like that want anything to do with you? I don't mean to be rude, Melvin, especially since you've done such a marvelous job for me, but let's face it. You stink! When's the last time you took a shower? Look at the way you live, like a rat hiding in a wall."

"You're a liar," I shouted. "Elle wouldn't do that."

"Believe what you want," he sighed.

"How did you know?"

"How did I know what?"

"How to play me, so perfectly?"

"It was all in your book," Victor chuckled. "Every button that needed to be pushed was right there in *Vape Mania*. Your contempt for the Institute. Your fondness for little girls. That's what Elle was to you, after all, wasn't she? A little girl who literally went from jail bait to womanhood in your arms?"

"Don't be disgusting," I said.

"Mostly I just allowed you to talk yourself into it. You're the one who told me about Sandra. You're the one who gave Patty Down Syndrome. I thought that was a nice touch, by the way." I shook my head, trying to remember. "Melvin, I'm not here to shatter your delusions."

"Then what are you here for? To kill me?"

"I put some thought into that, but no," he said. "This?" and he waved his gun around. "This was just in case you tried to stab me with an e-cig or something. But you seem to be handling it well enough. If I put this away, are you going to stab me with an e-cig?"

"No," I said.

"Say it."

"I'm not going to stab you with an electronic cigarette." I pulled one out anyway, and had a vape from it. Victor put his gun in his jacket pocket. "Why even bother telling me all of this?" I asked.

"You want to get paid, don't you?" he said and he kicked the backpack and it slid toward me with a puff of dust.

"What's that?"

"A hundred thousand, as you requested."

I reached down and unzipped it, confirming it was stuffed with stacks of cash. "Okay," I blurted, baffled. "I don't want to sound unappreciative," I said, scratching the scar under my trilby, "but why? I thought you, I mean Vera was dead. I didn't expect to get paid. Why bother?"

"I'd like to think that it's because I'm a man of my word," he said, "but, of course, there's more to it than that. You saw my face. You know I was in on it. I couldn't leave you with a million questions swimming around in that head of yours. You might have gone completely mad trying to find me. The way I see it, there's really only two choices. The first choice is, fill in some blanks for you, get the young girl's death off your conscience and make you feel paid. Then all the waves splashing around in-between your ears can be settled and our secret will be safe. The other choice is, put you six feet in a hole; and that would be a shame, considering you were so *fucking* good at what you did. Why waste you? I may need you. You might be a freak but freaks aren't bad friends to have in my line of work. So, please, take the money before I change my mind. The contract has been fulfilled. The account has been settled." He stood up. "You're a vape maniac; you know that, right?"

"Yeah, I know it," I said bitterly.

"If you don't mind, I really do need some help climbing down out of here." I held Victor's leathery hand as he stepped through the trap. He gained his footing on the ladder and climbed down.

As he was walking away across the yard, I stuck my head out the little window and called after him. "They *were* bad guys. Weren't they?"

"Complete assholes," he called back. "You did the city a favor. Thank you for your service, Mr. Provario."

Okay, so I turned out to be the biggest schmuck on the planet, but I was a schmuck with a quarter of a million dollars. I used the backpack as a pillow as I slept on the plywood that night, believing Elle and I would meet again someday. I hope you get to meet her as well, my dear Yugo. Maybe she can be there with me when I meet you on the same park bench, the one where you and I first met. Maybe that will happen on a date and at a time that's the standard battery connector for an iClear dual coil tank. Wink wink. I'll be wearing a brand new wool felt derby and the most expensive London Fog that money can buy.

The next morning, I woke to the sound of Brandon knocking on the hatch. I pulled it away to see him standing on the ladder, looking up at me. "My Dads are home," he said. "They want to talk to you.'

I knew what was coming, so I put on my backpack full of cash and grabbed my valuables off the work table before I climbed down in the coat and hat that was still scorched and sooty.

"Do they want to kill me?" I asked as we walked down the porch.

"Actually, no," he said. "They're in pretty good moods. They just got their settlement from Good Year

173

as a matter of fact. You really lucked out."

"Of course they got their settlement," I said, patting the breast of my coat. "What would life be without puzzling instances of synchronicity?"

I was brought into the dining room, where both Mr. Biebermans sat at the darkly stained table. They were smiling, their eyes glowing like two men who had just come back from an Indian adventure that rekindled their relationship only to find out they were going to receive a huge chunk of money. "Our son tells us he's been renting you some space," the old Mr. Bieberman said and cleared his throat, "um, in the attic?"

"Your son has been most gracious," I said, tipping my hat to Brandon who stood next to me. "He's a real gentleman and a fine young man."

"There's no easy way to put this," the Asian Mr. Bieberman said, "so I'll just come right out and say it. You're going to have to leave."

"Yes, I know," I said. I considered for a moment unzipping my backpack and tossing a wad of money onto the table in compensation for all the damage I had done, but figured the last thing I wanted anyone who might come looking for me to know is that I left with a sack of cash. So instead, I reached into my pocket and took out the framed photo of the two Dads that I had gotten repaired for them, and I set it on the table. The three of them looked at it inquisitively but quickly decided to move past it without bothering to ask.

"How long will you need to move out?" the older Mr. Bieberman asked, surprised by how smoothly things were going.

"I can go," I said, "now."

"You can leave now?" the Asian Mr. Bieberman happily asked. "It's no problem?"

"I've appreciated your son's hospitality. He's very

mature for his age. And I apologize for, well, you know—"

"Don't worry about it," they jinxed each other.

"Well, okay then," I said and I turned and gave Brandon a hug, patting him on the back, and then I offered my hand to each Mr. Bieberman. Both of them shook it in that awful way that I hate, cupped and barely touching, but I wasn't going let anything bother me. "Well, nice to meet you," I said, tipping my trilby. Brandon walked me to the door and as I was leaving down the sidewalk, with the burned futon mattress still in the yard under the graffiti, he called out, "Take care bro!" and I said, "You too, BB," before the door closed.

I went to the Currency Exchange and purchased a single stamp and an envelope that I addressed to my sister Alice. I took my settlement check out, endorsed it, put it in the envelope along with a piece of paper, on which I merely wrote, "For Granmama," and I tossed it into a mailbox. I don't even know where the idea came from but I was fine with it. I would keep the blood money and my charity would wash away my sins. And Granmama can hang out in the buff as much as her heart desires.

Besides my new coat and hat, I have been very fugal, my dear Yugo. I've set up an e-juice factory in the boiler room of an arts center, and I have been living off of that. I'm saving my real money for a special occasion. I may have to take care of the matter of the possessed e-juice, however. From what I understand the best way to deal with the vaping dead is a double pneumonectomy. I will spare you the gory details.

Wink wink.

XOXOXO,
Your Enamored Melvin.